THE
DESPERATE DEPUTY
OF
COUGAR HILL

THE DESPERATE DEPUTY OF COUGAR HILL

LOUIS TRIMBLE

THORNDIKE
CHIVERS

This Large Print edition is published by Thorndike Press®, Waterville, Maine USA and by BBC Audiobooks, Ltd, Bath, England.

Published in 2004 in the U.S. by arrangement with Golden West Literary Agency.

Published in 2005 in the U.K. by arrangement with Golden West Literary Agency.

U.S. Hardcover 0-7862-7116-7 (Western)
U.K. Hardcover 1-4056-3230-5 (Chivers Large Print)
U.K. Softcover 1-4056-3231-3 (Camden Large Print)

The text of this Large Print edition is unabridged.
Other aspects of the book may vary from the original edition.

Set in 16 pt. Plantin.

Printed in the United States on permanent paper.

British Library Cataloguing-in-Publication Data available

Library of Congress Cataloging-in-Publication Data

Trimble, Louis, 1917–
 The desperate deputy of Cougar Hill / Louis Trimble.
  p. cm.
 ISBN 0-7862-7116-7 (lg. print : hc : alk. paper)
 1. Sheriffs — Fiction. 2. Bank robberies — Fiction.
 3. Large type books. I. Title.
 PS3570.R519D47 2004
  913′.54—dc22   2004058824

THE DESPERATE DEPUTY
OF
COUGAR HILL

I

Deputy Marshal Roy Cameron rode half-standing in the saddle as he peered ahead of his shadow cast long by the slant of the late summer sun. He frowned as he counted the handful of cattle grazing on the rich valley grass.

Usually he took pleasure in the sight of these sleek cows, but today one of his prime yearlings was missing, and he was remembering the five head he had lost over the past few months. His first thought was to ride onto the benchland that lay just to the east and to challenge the Dondee brothers. But the fact that this was a prime steer missing held him in check. The Dondees, like the other so-called miners in this part of Idaho Territory, never helped themselves to any but scrub stock.

As his roan gelding topped a low hill, Cameron rose higher in the stirrups. He had caught a flash of white against the green of the grassland. From this distance, the white looked like a beef lying down and he pushed the roan to a faster pace.

Abruptly, he reined in. He had located the missing steer.

Cameron was normally an easy-going man, accustomed until these past months to letting life carry him whichever way it chose. But some of this easy approach was learned rather than natural with him. Years back, he had taught himself the futility of letting the quick surges of wild anger control him, of using his gun or his fists before stopping to think.

But now he felt the almost forgotten anger rise, shaking him. Someone had wantonly and wastefully butchered the yearling steer. They had cut off a hind-quarter and slashed out the tenderloin and left the rest for the buzzards wheeling overhead in the deep blue of the late afternoon sky.

Then the steer had been turned over so that the hip carrying Cameron's R-in-C brand showed plainly. It was as if the man who had done this wanted the finder to be sure and know whose beef had been treated this way.

Cameron stared thoughtfully eastward, beyond the timbered slope that rose from the valley floor a short distance to his left. The benchlands, bare of all but scrub growth after many years of miners working on them, showed plainly. A few of those old-timers still remained, eking out a living from their claims. But most of the men who called themselves miners were drifters, and Cameron had seen little evidence of their doing much work. And among those he classed as drifters were the Dondee brothers. They had only been in this tucked away piece of central Idaho Territory a short while, but already he had had half a dozen run-ins with them — both out here and in the town of Cougar Hill. Even so, Cameron found it hard to imagine them or any other miners wantonly destroying an animal in such a way.

He sat tight to the saddle, fighting to regain control of himself. Finally he began to think more clearly, to reason the possibilities of this being deliberate. In his years as a lawman throughout a good piece of the west, Cameron had learned that many men disliked the law, but he had never known one who would have taken out that dislike in such a fashion — even when it would have been safe to do so. And, in the sense of Cameron being the law, it was safe enough here in the valley. His jurisdiction ran only as far as the edge of town. The nearest law that counted was the sheriff in the county seat a hundred miles away, over rugged mountains.

Cameron shook his head. If this had been done to get at him for his tough rule of the town, how could the man hope to gain any satisfaction? Cameron might simply ride away, leaving the steer to the buzzards and leaving the butcher to an empty victory. No, if it had been done to hooraw him, then it obviously wasn't a finished piece of business. There would be more to come. For the butcher to win, Cameron would have to learn who he was.

Slowly now, he rode forward, searching the lush, well-watered grass. It was too springy to show hoof marks, but a short distance from where the steer lay, a trail of drying blood began. At first Cameron thought the blood merely the drippings from the freshly killed meat, and he wondered at the butcher's carelessness. Then he realized that this was a deliberately laid trail, that the spatters were leading him toward the wagonroad that led to the benchlands. He had been right — the killing of the steer was only the beginning of this business.

He reached the wagonroad a quarter mile east of where it crossed the stage-coach road that came into Cougar valley from the south. Now hoofprints were plain, and the blood spatters stood out against the light-colored dirt like ugly starbursts.

Two horses, Cameron read from the sign. One carried a big man, the other carried one a good deal smaller. Not the Dondee brothers then. They were twins and Hale was only a little smaller than Jupe.

The sign disappeared suddenly. Cameron reined up and looked around in surprise. The hoofprints turned toward the rank grass that grew up between worn twin ruts that took off sharply southward. And those ruts marked the road that led to Rafe Arker's stump ranch.

But Rafe Arker was in prison, in Boise, a good three-day ride away. He had been there a year and a half, so that Cameron, who had come to the Cougar country just over fourteen months ago, had never seen him. But he had heard the name often enough. And he had heard so much about Rafe Arker that sometimes he had the feeling he knew the man.

Arker, they said, was a two-legged bull. A mountain of wild, angry muscle. He had run Marshal Balder's last two deputies away, one leaving with a smashed face, the other with three broken bones. He was said to have once beaten a cowhand half to

11

death for daring to ask Jenny Purcell to a dance, even though she wasn't Rafe Arker's woman and had never given him any encouragement.

But she was going to marry Roy Cameron. And whenever that was mentioned there was talk about what Rafe Arker would do when he came out of prison. The general opinion was that Roy Cameron, for all his quick toughness, wouldn't get off much better than the previous deputy marshals had — if Rafe let him live.

Cameron's eyes followed the rutted track through a stand of scrub pine and on to the mouth of a cut that wound between sloping, sage-covered hills. On the far side of the cut was Rafe Arker's rundown stump ranch. Cameron had been there once, to talk to Joe Farley, Arker's sidekick. Farley lived there, supposedly taking care of the place while Arker served out his term for having tried to raid a wagontrain westbound out of Boise. And, Cameron recalled, Farley was a fairly small man.

When was Rafe Arker due to be let out of prison? Cameron frowned thoughtfully, remembering the warnings he had received these past months. "Rafe won't just try to run you out of the country," he had been told a dozen times. "When he hears about you and Jenny Purcell, he'll try to kill you. And if anyone in these parts can do it, Rafe's the man."

Men had tried to kill him before, and he had scars to show for the attempts, Cameron thought wryly. And one reason he was still alive was his way of hunting the trouble before it came up behind his back. He set the roan on the rutted trail, riding slowly in case the sign should turn off in another direction. But it kept straight on, leading him through the stand of scrub pine and into the cut. The sun was nearly set now and the sage hills blocked off its light, making the kinking trail shadowy. Brightness still touched the far end where the hills broke abruptly away, but suddenly that disappeared, blotted out by a massive man astride a big palomino.

He had guessed right, Cameron realized. This could only be Rafe Arker. And he could only have laid down his trail deliberately to bring Cameron to him.

Cameron reached for his gun. His fingers stopped inches from the worn butt. The man ahead had twisted in the saddle so that he faced Cameron even while his horse continued to block the trail. A carbine was steady in his hands, the barrel held on a line with Cameron's middle.

"That's far enough, deputy," he rumbled. His voice was deep and rough and filled with obvious pleasure. "Lift your hands up where I can get a good look at them."

Cameron obliged. The anger he had felt back in the valley was gone. His mind worked carefully, studying, weighing the situation and the man blocking the trail ahead.

Then he heard another horseman move into position behind him and stop only a few paces away. He glanced back and saw the flat, unshaven face of Joe Farley. And now there was no doubt that the man ahead was Rafe Arker.

Boxed, Cameron thought in self-disgust. He had expected to be led all the way to the ranch itself. He had not looked for a trap to be sprung so quickly, so easily. But now he had let himself be caught in a crossfire like the simplest greenhorn. Caught by the man everybody claimed wanted to kill him.

Arker was as big as he had been described. He towered a good half head over Cameron's lean six feet. His body was heavy — his chest barrel thick, his legs in tight Levis like ax-hewn tree trunks. The pallor of his skin under a three-day growth of beard looked oddly out of place on his heavy features.

Cameron leaned forward in the saddle, but without dropping his hands. "All right," he said with deceptive softness, "you've got me here, Arker. Now tell me why."

"It's near supper time," Arker answered. "I figured you'd like a piece of prime beef to chew on." He guffawed and slapped one hand heavily on his thigh. "Hear that, Joe? I'm running me a new business — a butcher shop!" He laughed harder, obviously pleased with himself.

"That steer was worth fifty dollars on the hoof," Cameron said. "I'll give you a week to sweat the prison stink off you and earn me that much money."

Arker gaped at him and then laughed again. "You hear that, Joe?" he demanded. "The deputy here don't seem to know he ain't the law once he's past the edge of town."

"I know it," Cameron said quietly. "And when I get a beef butchered, I do the same as the rest of the ranchers in the valley — I handle the problem myself. Where there is no law, every man has to be his own. It's a fool thing, but until the valley men vote the marshal's jurisdiction bigger than just the town, or until they're willing to pay for a deputy sheriff out of the county seat, that's the way it'll stand."

He was talking almost aimlessly, not really concerned that Rafe Arker knew his opinion of the local law problem; and while he talked, Cameron made an effort to size up the mountainous man blocking his way. He was seeking a weakness, something that would give him an opening, let him move into the position of advantage. But from where Cameron sat, Arker seemed to have control of this game — he was both banker and dealer and the cards were falling the way he wanted them to.

"All right," Arker said with his gusty laugh, "you're your own law here, deputy. You handle your own problems out in the valley. Start handling," he gibed.

"I told you I'd give you a week to collect the fifty dollars," Cameron said.

Arker snorted. "Fifty dollars! You'll take what I choose to give you — and be glad it ain't a bullet in the brisket. Right now I'm handing you a warning. When you get back to town, pack your warbag and ride. You been in these parts long enough."

He aimed his voice behind Cameron. "All right, Joe, ride up and get his gun.

You, lawman, keep your hands right where they are."

Cameron heard Joe Farley start his horse forward. He knew what to expect — he could read it in Arker's eager expression. Once Joe Farley disarmed him, he would be easy prey to all the hoorawing tricks a man like Arker would know. Perhaps lassoed and made to run behind a loping horse. And when he was exhausted, held up by Farley while Arker exercised his fists. And finally roped belly down across the saddle and sent to town like a sack of grain. That or a variation on it would be Arker's idea of amusement.

The whole of it — the anticipated pleasure, the arrogant sureness of himself — these were plain on Arker's heavy features. And as Cameron watched the man, he thought he might finally have found the weakness he sought — that all-consuming arrogance. Arker was not the kind to imagine that anyone would try to run a bluff against the gun he held or against his massive strength. And, Cameron guessed, feeling this way Arker might let down his guard a little.

In a moment he would know, Cameron thought. He listened to Farley's horse move alongside the roan. From the edge of his eye, he saw Farley reach across the gap between them, maneuvering with his left hand for Cameron's forty-four.

Now Cameron touched the roan with his toes, nudging it softly at the elbows. Obediently the horse stepped backward, dancing in a graceful motion. Farley grunted in surprise as his fingers closed over air. Then he swore sharply as Cameron, behind him now, brought the tips of his reins down across the rump of Farley's gray horse. The startled animal leaped forward, nearly unseating Farley before he could pull upright from his leaning position.

Cameron laughed as he caught a glimpse of Arker's face. It was dull red with anger now because the only way he could shoot at Cameron was to risk hitting Farley. The gray was going through the cut in wild leaps, urged on by Cameron's second scouring of its rump with his reins. And now Arker began to curse as he sought to swing the palomino out of its sidewise position.

His yowl of anguish battered the air as the gray rammed a shoulder into the side of the dun. Farley, still not fully seated, clawed for support and caught Arker around the neck. For a moment they clung together as if in some grotesque dance. Finally Arker swung his carbine in blind, wild anger. The sight raked down over the gray's nose, and with a frightened whinny it leaped backwards. The saddle was snatched from under Farley and he was left, legs flapping, with his arms tight around Arker's neck.

With a heave that brought muscles pushing hard against his shirt, Arker threw Farley to one side. The smaller man struck the ground, rolled, and lay still. Arker lifted himself in the stirrups, controlling the palomino with one hand and bringing the carbine around with the other.

Cameron continued to dance the roan backwards until a twist in the cut hid him from Arker's view. A bullet whined harmlessly through the space where he had been a moment before. Now it was Cameron's turn to laugh and he let the sound float mockingly back into the cut.

Arker cried, "I warned you, lawman. You be out of town by the time I get there tonight. You got a choice — ride out alive, or get carried out dead!"

II

Cameron's laughter kept him company a good part of the way to town. But finally the pleasure at remembering what had happened back in the cut faded away and he let himself think of the real Rafe Arker and not the buffoon the man had appeared for a few moments.

Cameron did not doubt that Arker meant his threat. His pride had been trampled; he had been made to look a fool in front of Joe Farley. And he would doubtless be afraid of Cameron's telling the story all over Cougar Hill.

Cameron frowned at the thought of having to watch for Arker in town. These past fourteen months had been the easiest of his working life. The most excitement Cougar Hill managed to generate was the annual visit by the army purchasing agent and a crew of cavalry to pick up the horses and mules the government contracted for. Then Cameron had an occasional fight on his hands now and then on a Saturday night. But no one ever really got out of line in town, not even the Dondee brothers.

His reactions had been slow back there, Cameron realized. Otherwise he would never have let himself get boxed so easily. As for his getting away, he recognized that was due half to surprise. Rafe Arker had not expected him to make a play. He wondered just how much fat the months of easy living had coated his nerves with. Just how slow had he become?

He would find the answer when Rafe Arker came to town and made his challenge.

Dusk was settling down as Cameron reached the south limits of town. Up ahead he saw the weekly stage stopped in front of the hotel and he disappointed the roan by riding on past McTigue's livery barn. It was Cameron's chore to meet the stage every Thursday and he hurried his horse now. But when he was just short of Hill Avenue, the cross street running alongside the hotel, he saw Marshal Balder come out of the jail office and start down the board sidewalk and he reined up.

He started to turn the roan around when the last passenger stepping out of the stage halted him. Light spilling from the hotel lobby was barely enough to dent the dusk and Cameron found it hard to make out the man's features. But there was something in the way he held his lean body and in the way he walked that stirred a memory deep in Cameron's mind. He sought for a name to put with the memory but it eluded him. When the man disappeared into the lobby, Cameron could only turn the roan and ride slowly back down Main Street to the livery.

He was as concerned with his own failure to recall the man as he was with the man himself. It was part of a law officer's work to keep a file of names and faces in his mind. More than once over the years Cameron's recognition of a wanted criminal, or even of just a troublemaker, had saved problems from developing. But now, search as he would, he could bring nothing more than a feeling of uneasiness from his mind.

Tod Purcell, Jenny's eighteen-year-old nephew, was on duty at the livery and he came hurrying from the cubbyhole office to take the reins of Cameron's horse. His freckled face was flushed with excitement. "The stage driver says Rafe Arker got let out of prison three days ago, Roy. I thought I better warn you because . . ."

"Arker's already home," Cameron said. He dropped to the ground and patted the roan. "Give him a good dollop of oats tonight."

"You saw Rafe?" Tod demanded.

"That's right," Cameron nodded. He started up the board sidewalk, leaving the boy staring after him in obvious admiration for his casual attitude.

"You're faking it a little," Cameron gibed at himself. He was too old a hand at the law business to feel casual about someone like Rafe Arker. But at the same time he was realist enough to know the value of a public attitude such as this. And Tod Purcell would spread the word that he had had his first meeting with Arker and had come through without a scratch.

And he needed the kind of admiration a story like this would bring, Cameron admitted honestly to himself. Since his first months in Cougar Hill, he knew this was the country he had been looking for. Eleven years of drifting — cattle work along the border, mining in the mountains, and finally law work in Colorado and Wyoming and Montana — with the need to sink his roots growing greater with each passing season. And now he was prodding thirty and soon the settling down would grow harder as the drifting habit bit deeper.

As he had explained to Jenny Purcell that night they realized that they felt the same way about each other, "There comes a time when every man likes to have something to put his back against. That's why I put what money I had into the ranch and why most of my salary goes to it for quite a time yet. That means we won't be able to get married as quick as I'd like."

She had kissed him in her quick way and answered, laughing, "You'll be marshal soon, Roy, and then you can afford the ranch and me both."

Cameron had taken the deputy job here with the understanding that he would be first in line for the marshal's job when Balder retired. For a time, when that would happen made little difference, nor did it seem of great importance. But that all changed when Jenny agreed to become his wife; and now Cameron was encouraged when the town fathers showed open approval of his work. Because it would be men like McTigue, who owned the livery and the hay and feed store just to the north of it, and Marcus Stedman, the banker, and John Colby, his cashier — these and two or three others would decide if Cameron was the man they wanted to replace Balder. And as Balder grew more openly eager to retire, the attitudes of these men grew more important.

And yet Cameron was no man to curry

favor, and more than once he had ruffled feelings, stepped on toes. He had openly told the townsmen and the valley ranchers that their refusal to extend the jurisdiction of the local law beyond the town limits was foolish penny pinching, and he made it clear that as marshal one of his first moves would be to fight for spreading the law through the entire Cougar valley country.

But they were fair-minded men for the most part, Cameron admitted. They knew that as the valley settled, the law would have to become stronger. And their concern at getting the right man stemmed from this realization.

He passed the Hay and Feed, the barber shop and bath house, the smaller of the two mercantile stores, and stopped on the corner of Hill Avenue. His handling of Rafe Arker just might be the final test, he thought.

Crossing Hill, he passed in front of the hotel, and momentarily he forgot Rafe Arker as memory of the stranger returned to him. He sought again to place the man, and again he failed. Frowning, he walked on toward the jail building.

It was quiet, but no more so than usual on a Thursday night. Darkness had shouldered aside the last of the evening light and there

25

was a hint of fall in the cool air that drifted down from the hills. As Cameron passed the weedy vacant lot that separated the hotel from the jail, the lamps came alight in the Widow Crotty's boarding house to the north. Across the street, light already came from Jenny Purcell's Café and from the bank just south of it. The end of the month, Cameron thought. Stedman and Colby would be working late for a night or two.

The jail office door was open and he turned in, finding Balder bent over a pile of paperwork on his desk. Balder looked up with a frown. "You're late tonight." His voice held a meaningless gruffness. He was a small man, dried with age like a California raisin grape, and uncompromising in his beliefs. But he seldom interfered with Cameron's handling of the law, even when it went against his ways.

Cameron said quietly, "I was talking to Rafe Arker."

Balder showed little surprise. "The stage driver was noising it around that Rafe got let out of the penitentiary. I was wondering when he'd get back here." The interest in his voice was obvious. "He give you any trouble?"

Cameron told him briefly what had

26

happened. Balder grunted. "Rafe's a fool in some ways. He don't know when to quit when he's ahead. He'll do everything he can to run you out of this country. He'll try to make you look bad so you'll have to pack up and ride. My advice is — make the first move. Every time he comes to town, roust him hard."

Cameron shook his head. "What happened today is valley business, and separate from my job here. If Arker starts trouble in town, then I'll use my authority. But I don't intend to roust him until he gives me a reason."

"He threatened you, ain't that reason enough? And he's been in prison," Balder snapped.

This was the major disagreement between the two men. Balder believed firmly that a leopard could never change its spots. That once a man had been in prison, the mark would be on him forever. And that a man who consorted with criminals or criminal types was infected and would always have to be watched. Tod Purcell and some other growing boys had ridden with Rafe Arker when his greatest crime was bullying; and though they had all straightened out quickly enough and left when his true nature became plain, Balder refused to trust any of them.

"You keep Rafe reminded where he's been and he won't be so eager to do something that'll get him put back there," Balder went on in a sharp tone. "The same thing goes for his friends. Make them know what being a jailbird is like."

Cameron had no desire to rake through the ashes of an old argument and so he said nothing. Balder glared challengingly at him. "Unless you don't figure you can stand up to Rafe," he snapped. "He ran my last two deputies out."

"So I heard — a dozen times," Cameron answered dryly. "I've faced up to men as big. I think I can handle him."

Balder made a snorting sound. "If you aim to prove who's boss by outdrawing him, you're wasting your time. Everybody knows you got the fastest draw around here. The town won't think you a hero for running Rafe away on the end of a six-shooter. Especially when the law says that nobody but you and me can carry a gun inside the city limits.

"If you want to put Rafe down and keep him down, you'll have to whip him with your hands," Balder went on. "And that's a chore many a man has tried but none ever finished. Just remember that, because Rafe'll try to make you fight him — no holds barred. If he gets you in that position and you use your gun instead, the whole town'll think you're afraid."

He paused and added heavily, "If that happens, I won't have any choice but to find me another deputy."

"I'll worry about it when the time comes," Cameron said. "Right now I want some supper."

Balder pushed the paperwork aside. "So do I," he said. In a characteristic sudden change of mood, he grinned at Cameron. "I'd like to have seen Farley draped all over Rafe there in the cut!"

"It's not something Arker will forget quickly," Cameron said. With a nod, he went out. He stopped on the edge of the board sidewalk and automatically glanced both ways along the dusty street. Things were still quiet, with no lights south of Hill except for the two saloons on the west side and, far down, the livery on the east.

He was about to start on again when a tall, slender figure came out of the hotel and crossed diagonally to the southwest corner. He walked just beyond the range of lamplight spilling from the bank, so Cameron could make out little detail. But the memory brought back by the way the man carried himself, the way he moved,

29

was even stronger than before.

The sound of singing came softly from the north. The Widow Crotty was playing the organ and her determined contralto almost drowned out the music. Cameron smiled. The Widow was holding her Thursday night singfest, as she called it, and all of her boarders except Cameron would be grouped around the organ, not to mention other town and valley people she had managed to corral, he thought.

Then the name of the song being sung struck him. It was *Lorinda.* And now the memory of Saxton Larabee came sharply to his mind. Memories of the times they had ridden together, drunk together, fought together. Sax was a little older, just enough to have been in the war near its end. He had a good voice and he had sung *Lorinda* a lot, had whistled it softly many a time when he rode night herd. But most of all, Cameron remembered him singing it softly and sadly in his cell at the Colorado prison.

This was a memory Cameron tried to keep far back in his mind, but there were times when it refused to stay there. A time like now — because he knew who the stranger reminded him of. In size and build, in the way he walked and held himself the man could have been Sax Larabee.

Cameron laughed shortly, mocking himself. To think that a man like Sax Larabee would come to an isolated mountain town such as Cougar Hill was absurd. His concern about Rafe Arker was making him dream up ghosts, Cameron thought. Sax Larabee was part of a past dead and buried all these years. It was foolishness to think that past could come to life again.

Moving quickly now, as if to escape from the song drifting down to him, Cameron went into Jenny's café. The supper hour was almost over and the only customer was Obed Beggs, perched on one of the three counter stools. The room was small, with only four tables besides the counter, and the fragrant odors of stew, freshly boiled coffee, and newly baked pie were packed tightly in the air. Cameron nodded pleasantly to Obed Beggs and sniffed hungrily as he slid onto a stool.

Jenny Purcell was behind the counter, the sleeves of her plain green dress pushed to her elbows and her hands in a full dishpan. Cameron looked down for a moment at the crown of her wheat-blond hair, and then she lifted her head and touched him with the warmth of her smile. She was a pretty woman with hauntingly large gray eyes, but their beauty was darkened by a shadow of concern. Cameron guessed she had heard the rumor about Rafe Arker.

"I saved a piece of apple pie for you," she said in her husky voice.

"And after you eat it, you'll be so contented you won't be able to say no to a favor I got to ask," Obed Beggs put in. He was a tall, spare old man, owner of the biggest cattle and mule ranch in the valley. It was a piece of his range Cameron had bought.

"I know," Cameron said, "you want me to help with the roundup next week."

"I got about everybody else except for a few drifters," Obed said. His eyes gleamed. "And I'll need just about twice as many riders as we got people in this Cougar country. Did you hear that the army wants three times more horses and mules than they ever bought from us before?"

"I heard," Cameron said.

"Those bankers'll have to be working nights for quite a while to keep track of all the gold there'll be in these parts," Obed chortled. "Think of all the mortgages that'll get reduced! And all the little debts men can pay off with the money they make in the roundup. It'll be the easiest winter most folks ever had to look forward to."

Jenny smiled at Cameron. "I offered to turn the café over to Manuel and help out, and I think Obed's about to agree."

"I'll take anybody can sit a horse," Obed said. "When the ranchers put me in charge of this shindig I didn't know what I was getting into. I thought the way my horses and mules are scattered all over summer range was bad enough, but you should try to find some of he critters Val Vaught and Toby Landon own."

He gulped down his coffee and stood up. "Try to find time from your law work, Roy. Now I better get or the Widow Crotty'll think I'm dodging her singamajig." He hurried out.

Cameron watched Jenny dry her hands and then move gracefully about in the small space behind the counter. She brought him a bowl of stew and thick slices of homemade bread. Then she stepped back and silently watched him eat.

"You heard about Rafe Arker?" Cameron asked. She nodded and he said, "If you're worried he might come here, I can get you a gun."

"I have one under the counter," Jenny said. "But Rafe would never hurt me personally."

"Then you're afraid of what he might try to do to me?"

She touched his hand with the warm tips of her fingers. "I'm afraid," she admitted. She shook her head as if to deny her own words. "I'm not afraid as long as you can face him. I've seen you fight those big cavalrymen. It isn't that. It's what could happen when you turn your back. Rafe has never cared how he gets what he wants, just so that he gets it."

She could be talking about Sax Larabee in the old days, Cameron thought. And he felt a stir of anger directed at himself for not being able to keep from thinking about Sax Larabee.

Before he could answer Jenny, the door burst open. Tod Purcell staggered in, his freckles standing out with excitement and his mouth open while he sucked in air.

"Rafe's come to the Silver Strike with Joe Farley, Roy. And they're causing trouble already!"

Cameron spooned up a mouthful of stew and waited. Tod caught his breath. "Both of them refused to check their guns with the barkeep. More than half the customers have already got up and left. The swamper came and told me to find you."

Cameron swallowed his stew and slid off

the stool. "Is Rafe drinking?"

"Just one whiskey, I was told."

Cameron nodded at the stew. "Keep it hot; I'll be back in a while."

"I'll do that," Jenny said, and turned quickly away.

III

Cameron strode down the board sidewalk toward the Silver Strike Saloon. It was the most southerly of the two on Main Street, and the place that caused most of the trouble on a Saturday night. Most of the drifters and miners patronized it, while the sawmill workers and the settled cowhands and the small ranchers went to the Cattleman's Bar three doors to the north. The well-to-do, both from town and valley, did their drinking in the hotel bar.

But for all that the hotel bar was quietest; Cameron checked it with the same thoroughness he checked the other saloons. And he was as insistent that Obed Beggs check his gun as he was that the poorest drifter do so. That was Balder's law — no one but the marshal and his deputy carried hardware inside the town limits.

Tod Purcell trotted alongside Cameron. "What do you figure on doing, Roy?"

"Make Rafe Arker and Joe Farley check their guns."

"And if they don't?"

"Then they get out of town the same as anyone else. If they kick up a fuss, they'll have to cool off in a cell. They're no different from other people."

Cameron stopped just short of the heavy plank door of the saloon. "You get back to the livery," he said.

"There are a few in there that'll side with Rafe if they get a chance," Tod said.

"I expected as much," Cameron admitted. "But if the law had to have outside help everywhere it went, it wouldn't be much force. This is my job. If I can't do it, I'd better quit being the law."

Tod moved reluctantly away. Cameron watched until he was back in the livery, safely out of the way. Then he started toward the door. He stopped to loosen his gun and to set his hat. He felt no fear and wondered at his own hesitancy. Sooner or later, he would have to face down Rafe Arker. It was just another lawing chore that had to be done.

But the question came sharply to his mind: Had he slowed down after these months of quiet living? Fear that he might have, he realized, explained Balder's attitude and Tod Purcell's hesitancy.

It was a question that he knew only one way to answer. He pushed open the door and stepped into the saloon. Kicking the door shut with his boot-heel, he stood quietly, his head moving from side to side as he measured the men in the room.

It was a small place with a short bar at one end, a cleared space for dancing on those rare occasions when hurdy-gurdy girls trouped through town, and room for three card tables at the back. All three tables were occupied, two with card players. The third held the Dondee brothers who were too busy staring at Cameron to worry about the cards and chips in front of them.

Cameron was surprised to find them here on a week night but he gave no sign of his interest. He was more concerned with Rafe Arker. He and Joe Farley were bellied up to the bar, Rafe in a position to have his broad back turned contemptuously toward the door, and to have his .44 visible on his hip.

Two other men at the bar were backed as far from Arker as they could get without leaving. Cameron noted that the younger one was Nick Ramey, one of Obed Beggs' hands. The other was a stranger to him.

The barkeep was a sallow-faced man with an oversized mustache covering his upper lip. He was pouring Ramey a drink. When he finished, he backed against his liquor rack and watched Cameron.

Rafe Arker kept his back to the door. "Get out, lawman," he ordered in his heavy voice. "This is a private party."

"The law says you check your guns when you first hit town," Cameron stated in his quiet way. "Now both of you draw slow and easy. I want to see that hardware on the bartop. Now!"

Silence came down over the small room. Cameron stood apparently relaxed. But inside he was taut, holding himself ready for any move Arker might make. What the man did at this moment would determine the course of things from now on.

Arker straightened up and turned slowly. His right side was next to the bar now and he stepped away to give his gun arm room.

"My gun stays with me," he challenged.

Jupe Dondee called out, "Better watch yourself, mister. The deputy here's a real gunslick."

Cameron's glance moved around the room, lingering longest on Nick Ramey. From the expressions he saw he realized that Balder had been right. It would mean nothing for him to beat Rafe Arker to the draw. He would have to prove his authority over this mountain of a man with his fists.

Arker had finished his turn and now it

was Cameron's right to move. He started slowly forward, his eyes fixed on Arker. The big man was motionless, his massive torso bent slightly forward in a gunfighter's crouch, his fingers just clear of his gun butt.

Cameron kept his eyes on Rafe Arker's face, not on his hand. He had learned long ago that a man's eyes and expression revealed more of his intent than a hand motion. And always the quick blink or the sudden fixed stare, the tautness around the mouth or the uncontrollable twitch of a muscle — one of these preceded the draw by a fraction of time.

Cameron walked with his arm crooked slightly at the elbow, his fingertips brushing his gun butt. His stride was slow-paced, steady. With each forward step he made, the silence in the saloon thickened until it was like a solid wall wrapping itself around himself and around Rafe Arker, a cocoon that cut them off from awareness of their surroundings.

Arker and Cameron had been a good twenty feet apart before. Now the distance between them was six feet. Cameron lifted his foot for another step. He saw the tell-tale movement from Rafe Arker — the involuntary flick of the man's tongue across dry lips. At almost the same instant, Arker dove for leather. He stopped his draw abruptly, his .44 barely more than half clear of its holster. Surprise flooded his expression as he stared at Cameron's gun, drawn and aimed steadily for his belly.

"Hardware on the bar, butt first," Cameron said. His words dropped softly into the thick pool of quiet. "You first, Arker."

With aching slowness, Rafe Arker pulled his gun free. He turned and with the same slowness, laid the gun on the bar top. A sigh rustled through the watching men as he lifted his hand, empty, and stepped back.

"Your turn, Farley," Cameron commanded.

Joe Farley followed Arker's lead, his small body stiff with frustration. As he moved away from the bar, his lips moved jerkily, throwing words at Arker that were too soft for anyone else to hear.

Arker grunted and stared fixedly at Cameron.

From the rear of the room, Jupe Dondee called again, "I told you to watch yourself, mister."

The mocking twist was back on Rafe Arker's mouth. "So the law is faster with a gun. That don't prove nothing."

41

Cameron could feel the challenge in the words bring all eyes toward him. He had resigned himself to the fight with Arker and for the moment was not concerned about it. But he was puzzled at the way this affair was going. Even though Arker had obviously been surprised at the speed of Cameron's draw, he had not acted as if he expected to win a gun duel. Rather, Cameron thought, he had acted as if he expected to lose it.

Cameron could not rid himself of the feeling that each move Rafe Arker had made — from the butchering of the steer to the laying of his gun on the bar — had been carefully planned in advance. Planned to force Cameron into moves he had no desire to make. He had the sensation of playing a game of chess against an expert. And yet it was impossible to believe that Rafe Arker was capable of planning one move ahead, let alone a half dozen.

Cameron took a backward step. "Take those guns," he ordered the barkeep. They disappeared from the bartop and Cameron holstered his own weapon. He unbuckled his belt and let it drop to the floor. Pushing it aside with a foot, he took off his hat and sailed it on top of the gun and belt. Each move was made slowly and deliberately.

"It's time you learned what the law is," Cameron said softly.

And now it was Arker's turn to hesitate. Clearly he had not expected Cameron to accept his challenge, to meet him in hand-to-hand combat. Surprise flickered into his eyes and then drained away, letting the contempt appear again.

"That's an old trick," he rumbled. "After I whip you, the marshal hauls me to jail for resisting a law officer."

Cameron's answer was to unpin the star from his vest and to drop it into the crown of his hat. Again Arker showed momentary surprise. Then he laughed.

Cameron stood quietly. Again he was waiting for the signal that would tell him Arker was going to make his move. This time Cameron expected a bull rush, an attempt to catch him in those thick arms — a catch-as-catch-can, no-holds-barred kind of wrestling that would let Arker take full advantage of his size and weight.

The street door opened. Momentarily all eyes turned in that direction. Cameron followed suit, wanting to make sure that this was not a threat aimed at his unprotected back.

The sight of the man quietly closing the door behind himself was a shock that froze

Cameron, briefly blotting out everything else around him. The slim, sharply chiseled features with the long upper lip, the widow's peak of black hair coming off a high forehead, the sardonic glint in the black eyes — these Cameron could never have forgotten.

Sax Larabee! And Cameron knew that the ghost of the long dead past had come to life. The memories he had sought so long to bury were no longer memories. They were reality.

The sound of a foot scuffing on bare boards jerked Cameron around. Arker was coming toward him. He moved his huge bulk with surprising speed, and not as Cameron expected in a bull rush, but lightly, on his toes like a boxer. Before Cameron could shift his full attention from Sax Larabee to Arker, the big man was on him.

Cameron stepped back, but not quickly enough. Arker drove out his left fist, slamming rock-hard knuckles against Cameron's temple. He felt the skin peel back and the force of the blow sent him off balance. He staggered against a table and crashed with it to the floor. He rolled and came to his knees.

Close by, Jupe Dondee laughed with

deep pleasure. Cameron staggered to his feet, shaking his head. Rafe Arker was a blur filling the cleared space between the bar and the tables. Cameron stayed where he was, sucking in air, fighting to clear the mist from in front of his eyes. Another minute, he thought, and he would be able to see again; he would be free of the paralysis gripping his muscles.

Then Jupe Dondee laughed a second time. Cameron felt hands against his back, felt himself pushed roughly forward to where Rafe Arker waited. He saw Arker's grin swim at him through a reddish haze. He saw the big fist driving for his face. He caught the blow on the forearm, reacting by instinct. At the same time he pivoted to avoid the body blow that should follow that first fist. He felt the jar of bone against his arm and felt the wind of Arker's other fist as it slid past his belt buckle. Then his senses cleared.

Arker had thrown both punches hard, driving them with his legs as well as his shoulders as he sought for the quick kill, and so he was leaning slightly forward, a hairline off balance. And now it was Cameron's turn. He stepped in and hit Arker twice, under the eye and across the bridge of the nose. He took a punishing fist on the shoulder and then stepped back out of range.

The blow to the nose had hurt, Cameron saw. Arker's eyes were watering. Again Cameron moved in. He feinted for Arker's eyes with his left, and when Arker's guard came up he drove under it to smash viciously at the nose again. He twisted as he struck, tearing skin and crunching cartilage. Arker's mouth came open and he flailed out wildly. Cameron back-pedaled, drawing Arker after him. The big man kept up his wild swinging, obviously hoping to send Cameron down again.

Cameron had fought men bigger than himself before. He knew from experience that once inside Arker's crushing arms he would be helpless. He also knew that the big man was liable to depend too much on his strength, to forget in the driving tempo of a fight whatever rudiments of boxing he might know. And as Cameron hoped, it was this way with Rafe Arker.

Cameron sidestepped Arker's rushes. Each time Arker charged by, he reached out and flicked a fist at the man's unprotected face. Ripping knuckles caught Arker full on the mouth, splitting his lips. Twisting fists slashed at the exposed eyes, tore unmercifully at the already battered nose.

Arker caught him a second time on the temple. But his blows lacked force now, and Cameron was able to come back in quickly, under Arker's guard, to rip again and again at the bleeding, torn features. And now Cameron stepped in tight and began to whip his blows into Arker's body. His fists sank into muscle made flabby by a prison diet. Arker's mouth came open in pain as Cameron scored twice under the heart.

And now Arker gave ground. Slowly, steadily, his big body kept backing away, yielding each inch reluctantly. Cameron shifted his aim, moving from Arker's torso to his face and back again. His knuckles began slipping on Arker's blood, and now it was only a matter of time.

Rafe Arker growled from deep in his throat. He continued to lash out with his huge fists. Half blinded, he swung his great trunk like a wild animal. For all the pain that rode him, for all that his eyes were swollen half shut, his nose and mouth a mass of flowing blood, he still moved with surprising grace and speed. And suddenly his massive fist caught Cameron on the forehead. He tried to lean away from the next blow. It took him under the ear and spun him, dazed, to the floor.

He was up quickly to one knee, blinking his eyes to clear them. He saw Arker lean forward to focus his gaze and then come charging down, his legs driving. The way he ran told Cameron he intended using his boots. Cameron drove himself upward with a powerful thrust of his legs. He caught Arker at the beltline with his shoulder. The force of his charge sent Arker backward, arms flailing. His back hit the bar, sending glasses dancing. Cameron straightened up and stepped back far enough to give himself room to swing. He lifted his arm and let it drop down again.

Rafe Arker was sagging at the knees. His expression was empty. Cameron stepped back again. There was nothing here for him to fight. He simply stood and waited while Arker slid slowly down to his knees and then fell forward to bury his face against the rough boards of the floor.

Cameron walked to his small pile of gear and put it on. Sax Larabee spoke up and he turned, meeting the man's gaze full face. "That was a fine fight. I'll stand you a drink." There was no hint of recognition in his eyes; none in his voice.

"No," Cameron said. He turned away and strode to the table where Jupe and Hale Dondee sat.

They were twins, look-alikes except that Jupe wore a shaggy black beard and Hale just seemed to have forgotten to shave. They were short, solid men; and for all that they professed to be experienced miners, they dressed and walked like men more accustomed to a saddle than a pick and shovel.

"Next time I want help in a fight, I'll ask for it," Cameron said softly.

Jupe Dondee's truculent glare shifted away. Cameron said, "And another warning. Keep away from my cows."

"Now look here," Jupe protested. "You never proved nothing on me and Hale. We don't . . ."

"One of these days I will prove something," Cameron interrupted. "And just remember — out in the valley I'm no more bound by the law than you are." He swung away from the mixture of fear and anger that leaped into both men's eyes. Not bothering to look at Rafe Arker still lying motionless on the floor, he walked outside.

The night had begun to cool, and there was a hint of fall in the air that rolled down from the mountains. Cameron hunched his shoulders and winced as the movement pulled bruised flesh. He walked slowly up the empty board sidewalk.

49

Light still showed from Jenny's Café, and Cameron knew that she was waiting for him. He would go there and have his piece of pie, he decided.

Then he would go back to the jail office and wait for Sax Larabee and the past to come to him.

IV

Jenny had kept both the stew and a piece of apple pie hot for Cameron. The café was officially closed for the night and so they had it to themselves. Cameron ate slowly, savoring the food and the obvious concern for him Jenny showed.

"Somebody will spread the word about what happened tonight, and you'll be a hero for a day or two," she said.

"It's foolishness," Cameron answered, "but of a kind that never hurts the law's reputation." He was shaping a cigarette to go with his coffee and he glanced up at her. "You sound almost bitter."

"I was just thinking that the bigger a fighting man's reputation, the more people want to best him."

"In the Cougar country, I don't have to worry about anyone but Rafe Arker," Cameron smiled. "And he won't be bothering anybody for a few days."

Jenny shook her head. "I don't know why but I'm afraid for you — more than I was before you fought Rafe."

With an effort, she laughed away her frown and leaned over the counter to kiss Cameron. "I sound like a biddy hen, don't I? But you won't have to listen to me much longer. I promised Matilda Crotty I'd go to her singfest."

The Widow Crotty's was quiet as Cameron escorted Jenny to the front door. Through the diamond glass panes, he could see the singing group seated in the parlor, eating applesauce cake with gobbets of fresh whipped cream on top. For a moment Cameron envied these people the quietness of their lives. But as he turned to walk back to the jail office, the feeling vanished. When he first decided to become a lawman, he knew what the future would hold for him. And only seldom had he ever regretted his decision, and then not for long.

But tonight the feeling came back, and he knew that it was because of Sax Larabee. He and Sax, wild kids drifting about the ranges of the west, working hard and playing hard, burning up their energies with the enthusiasm and thoughtlessness of healthy young animals.

And then Cameron became aware of the change in Sax. Older and with a little more education than Cameron possessed — and a good deal more than most of the others they rode with had — he began to fret at his lack of success. A bitterness seemed to grow in him as he came to realize that the mere fact he was Sax Larabee was not enough to bring him more than other people.

Cameron still remembered with sharp clarity the night Sax's feelings came to a head. With two friends and two strangers, they were drifting south after working a roundup in the San Juan country of Colorado. They were camped on the upper Rio Grande and had just finished supper when Sax stood up, a cheroot clamped between his teeth and his hat thumbed back to show the widow's peak in his black hair.

Cameron would never forget the hell-for-leather grin on Sax's lips nor the wild glint in his dark eyes. "That roundup left a lot of money in the Alamoso bank," he said suddenly. "You all know money's the root of evil. Now I'm a man who's always been hellbent against evil, and I aim to change the situation back there in town."

Skeet Ryan laughed and got to his feet. "I'm with you, preacher."

Toby Callow and the other two, whose names Cameron could never remember, joined Sax Larabee as well. Cameron stood up too, finally, but with the intent of riding the other way. It was a simple parting, with no arguing on Sax's part. He said, "I'll be seeing you, Roy," and turned away. It had been an empty ride south for Cameron, knowing as he did that even if they met again things could never be quite the same between them.

He put up for the night with a sheepherder camped on the river just north of the border with New Mexico Territory. From there he drifted, not coming back to Colorado for nearly two months. And when he did, he was arrested.

He learned that Sax and Toby and one of the drifters had been arrested on their way out of the bank. Skeet and the other drifter had fought their way free and ridden off. Since Cameron was known to have ridden with Sax and Skeet, the law decided he was the second man and wanted posters were put out.

The sheriff was fair enough with Cameron. He sent a deputy to find the sheepherder Cameron claimed to have spent the night with. But the man had gone into the hills, and Cameron was tried and sentenced and locked in the penitentiary for three months before the evidence to clear him came.

The law made its manners and apologized. But that nor anything else could wipe out the grim memories of prison. Nor of Sax Larabee.

It was Sax's claim that Cameron had doubled back that night and warned the authorities, and that they had given him his term in prison to keep the gang from knowing this and so planning a future revenge. Cameron's quick release confirmed his opinion, despite anything Cameron or the sheriff could say.

And when Cameron walked past the cells on his way out, Sax called, "I'll find you, Roy. And when I do, I'll pay you back for every day of the three years they're keeping me in here."

Cameron put the memories deep in his mind and rode west. He worked a ranch here and there and tried his hand at mining, and finally he accepted a job as deputy. It took only a little while for him to realize that this was the kind of work he wanted, and to protect himself he told the old lawman he worked for the story of his past.

The sheriff cursed him for a fool. "People talk a lot about honesty, but they won't love you for showing it, son. You're shaping into a good law officer. But you'll never keep a job as one in any decent town as long as you tell folks you was in prison. By the time they get around to believing you were there by accident, they'll already have you down as a scoundrel who made fools of them. So forget what you was — just think about what you are."

It was advice Cameron took. As he drifted north and west, he built a solid reputation around himself. Even so, Balder asked a lot of questions when he talked to Cameron about being his deputy with an eye to the main job in a short while. Cameron answered the questions readily enough, but he blotted out the years that Sax Larabee had touched.

But, he thought now, that was like writing on paper with your pen dipped in milk. The words were still there even if they were invisible. And when someone touched heat to the paper, those words came out bold and clear. It was that way here — Sax Larabee's coming was the heat that was going to make Cameron's past stand out for everyone to read.

Cameron walked into the jail office and settled behind the desk. The pile of paper work was still there and he thought of Marshal Balder. What would he think when Sax Larabee exposed Cameron's past? In fourteen months Cameron had come to know the old man well. He would be fair — he would ask Cameron for the truth. But once he heard it, that would be the end of Cameron's future. Balder, Stedman, Colby, McTigue — they would all react the same way. Jenny? He suspected that she would stand by him; she would believe he had been jailed unfairly before he could even tell her as much. But what would such a revelation do to Tod, and to other boys like him? Growing out of boyhood but not quite yet men, they were balanced on the tightrope between what Cameron represented as a lawman and the lure of the wild life. Cameron was aware of the admiration many local boys had for him, Tod in particular. More than anything, he was afraid of the effect Sax's story might have on them.

Cameron realized he was staring at the doorway. Sax Larabee would be coming through there soon, coming to remind Cameron of his threat of so many years ago — coming to lay out the past for everyone to see. Slowly Cameron pulled out his gun and laid it on the desk top, ready to his hand.

He rolled and lit a cigarette. He laid his hand on the gun, finger resting on the trigger guard, thumb ready to the hammer. He heard the light, rapid footfalls. His gun came up and steadied, aimed at the doorway.

Sax Larabee appeared. He stopped, framing himself momentarily in the doorway. His dark eyes touched the gun and moved on to Cameron's face.

"You haven't changed that much," Sax Larabee said.

"No," Cameron agreed. With a sudden motion, he thrust the gun back in its holster.

Sax Larabee smiled and moved with his catlike grace to the one extra chair. He looked almost the same, despite the long years that had flowed by. But then, Cameron thought, Sax was still a young man. And that deceptive slenderness would hide the same wire-rope muscles, just as his faintly mocking smile and saturnine expression hid the same shrewd brain, still honed as fine as a good barber's best razor.

Cameron had always been a little in awe of the speed with which Sax's brain worked. And a little surprised at the streak of malevolence that could turn Sax into a wild-eyed fury. Now he remembered those things and cold fear touched him.

Sax Larabee stretched his long legs,

selected a cheroot from a silver carrying case, and leaned back in the chair. "You got around over the years, Roy. But I hear you plan to stay here, become the local law, be a big rancher."

He lit his cheroot carefully. "You didn't leave that big ox of an Arker much to be proud of."

"I didn't intend to," Cameron said quietly.

"You did that to him because you're a lawman and he's fresh from prison. Is that what you want to do to me too, Roy? Is that the way you feel about me?"

"I feel nothing about you," Cameron said. "No more than I would about any other stranger. If you're here on legal business, I'll forget you. If you aren't, I'll see that you leave."

Sax Larabee's smile tilted his finely shaped lips. "No," he said. "No matter what I do, you won't roust me. Not you, Roy. And you won't let the marshal do anything either."

The threat was plain enough but Cameron chose to ignore it. "What did you come here for?" he demanded.

Sax laughed. "I'm a businessman. I deal in properties — mines, ranches, farms. I've made a lot of money since those three years ended." He continued to smile but his eyes held the cold darkness of water deep in a well.

"This is a little man's country. There's nothing here for you."

"I'll judge that," Sax answered. "I may find just the thing I'm looking for. And if I do, I might want some help — for old time's sake."

He rose. "Until then I'll be just another stranger — as you put it. Unless you want things otherwise. Unless you want to introduce me around as an old friend — from, say, Alamoso."

The wild, hot anger washed up in Cameron, bringing him to his feet before he could get himself under control. He took a step toward Sax Larabee and stopped. Sax was still smiling but the darkness in his eyes had turned colder, splintered into shards of black ice. They froze Cameron.

"You can whip me — with a gun or your fists," Sax said. "But don't try it. Don't try anything with me. I'll leave your country when I'm ready. How I leave it and what I leave behind — that depends on you."

V

Cameron roused himself and turned away from the door Sax Larabee had just gone through. He still had his night rounds to make and so he went out the rear door and on down the alley. He checked carefully, but automatically, probing each shadow, testing the locks on windows and doors. But his mind was on Sax Larabee, not on this routine.

He was trying to find Sax's reasons for having come here. Not just to find him, Cameron was sure. Knowing the man as he did, he guessed shrewdly that Larabee could have found him any time he chose. More than likely, Cameron decided, Sax had learned he was here and then had sought a way to capitalize on that knowledge — to get his revenge and to make money at the same time.

And how long, he wondered, had Sax Larabee waited for just this opportunity, waited for the time when Cameron had achieved enough to make him worth destroying?

But that didn't matter now. What did

matter was Sax Larabee's presence here, and the other reason for it. Because obviously he had a plan of some kind. And more obviously, he expected to use Cameron to make his plan work.

Cameron steadied the anger threatening him again. He had to keep his mind clear. He had to think, to try to find a way to outmaneuver Sax Larabee.

But when he thought of going up against that cold, deadly mind, the finger of hopelessness laid its weight on him. Whatever he might try, Sax would inevitably be there first, waiting to block him. Waiting to use him and then to destroy him.

Finally Cameron realized that there was only one possible line of action he could take right now. He would follow the usual pattern when a stranger came to town and stayed.

And so in the two days that followed, he kept himself informed on Sax's comings and goings. In the mornings, when Cameron was asleep, Balder took note of the places Sax went, the people he spoke to. In the afternoons, Cameron did the work himself, with volunteer help from Tod Purcell.

According to Balder, Larabee usually appeared in midmorning and strolled around town, talking to the bankers or one of the other businessmen. Both days, Cameron saw him lunching with Stedman; and on Friday evening he spent his time in a poker game with McTigue, Judge Bellow, and Roper, who owned the bigger mercantile store.

Saturday afternoon, Cameron watched Sax stroll over to the bank with Stedman, talk briefly, and then leave. Cameron waited until Sax entered the hotel and then he walked into Stedman's office.

"I notice that stranger talking to you quite a bit," Cameron said bluntly. "Is he here on business?"

Stedman was a long, bony man with bushy graying eyebrows over deep-set eyes. He let his eyebrows go up as he stared in mild surprise at Cameron. "I suppose it's your affair to find out," he said. But he sounded none too pleased.

"If you have a business deal going, don't think I'm trying to pry into it," Cameron said. "But a stranger is always the law's affair. There's more than one confidence man making his living from towns the size of ours."

Stedman acknowledged the point with a brief nod. "Mr. Larabee is interested in investing in some land," he said. "He's especially interested in the mines. I told him they were about played out, but he claims modern machinery has brought a fortune from more than one played-out mine. And he's been looking them over for himself."

The answers were almost always the same, no matter which businessman Cameron asked. Sax Larabee seemed to have legitimate interests and he talked knowledgeably enough about the subject of mining. He was, Cameron thought with grudging admiration, revealing nothing of his real reason for being here.

Cameron was having supper with Tod Purcell when the first glimmering of a useful idea came to him. Tod said, "That city man must have wore the skin off his tailbone these last two days. Both yesterday morning and this one, just before I go off duty, he's come in and rented a horse. According to the ledger, he stayed out four hours each time."

"Do you have any idea which way he went?" Cameron asked.

Tod chewed a mouthful of roast beef. "He never said, but tonight just before I come here I had to curry the horse he used this morning. McTigue got busy and left the job for me. I found pricklebush leaves around his fetlocks."

He glanced to the north. There high mountains enclosed the valley, running to the westward and a short distance east. "Seeing as he couldn't have had much place to ride except the southeast and south ends of the country and seeing as pricklebush don't grow anywhere but the hillsides up above your spread, I figure he must have gone that way."

Cameron laughed. "That's good reasoning," he said. He was thinking about the places where Sax Larabee might have ridden these past two mornings. But there were too many for him to find an easy answer. Besides his own place, a half dozen miners, including the Dondee brothers, worked in that area; Rafe Arker's stump ranch was there; and so was the cut-up land where Obed Beggs ran some of his scrub stock. Cameron could imagine no connection between Sax and Rafe Arker and Obed Beggs. That left the miners, and for a moment he wondered if the man could have been telling the businessmen the truth — if he really was interested in reworking old mines.

Tod said, "I don't reckon he's taken to visiting Rafe. Nick Ramey was out that way chousing strays this morning and he told me Rafe's still not moving around good. Joe Farley had to get a buckboard to pack him home the other night after the fight and he ain't been off his back since. He wouldn't be in any mood to welcome a stranger."

Cameron frowned. "Rafe Arker wasn't hurt that bad," he said flatly. He started to say more when Obed Beggs came over to their table and asked to sit down. Settled and with a plate of roast beef in front of him, Obed said, "I hear you mention Rafe Arker?"

Tod repeated what he'd told Cameron. Obed frowned. "I was hoping Rafe'd be up and about enough to help with the roundup." He grinned in his dry way at Cameron's surprised expression. "Sure, I know Rafe'd be more likely to help himself to the horses instead of running them in for the army to take, but I'm desperate. It's going to take every man in the valley riding from sunup to sundown to bring in all the stock them cavalry boys want. Sometimes I wish we hadn't bred such good horses and mules these past few years."

He looked at Tod. "I already told McTigue he either had to ride with us or work nights so you could come. He decided you're a better size to fit a horse." He chuckled. "Why, I even got that stranger to agree to join us for a few days. And he said he'd see if he couldn't talk some of them miners into putting in time."

Cameron saw that it was time to relieve Balder. He rose. "As I said, I'll give you the afternoons, Obed."

"It all helps," Obed said.

Cameron found Balder writing a letter. Finishing, the old man waved the paper around to dry the ink. "I wrote to Boise," he said, "about this stranger Larabee. He says he's from San Francisco in California, and maybe he is. But he talks like a man from southern Colorado or western Kansas to me. Billy Rogers from those parts is working in the sheriff's office in Boise and I'm asking him if he ever heard the name or saw a man looks like this Larabee."

Cameron busied himself checking his gun, not wanting Balder to see the concern he knew must show on his face. It had never occurred to him that the marshal would go this far investigating an apparently harmless stranger. This Rogers just might know of Sax Larabee and then there could be trouble that neither Cameron nor Sax could stop.

"From the way Stedman and the other

businessmen talk, he seems to be all right," Cameron said.

Balder glanced sharply at him. "You don't seem to think so — the time you put in checking on Larabee."

Cameron revealed part of the idea that had come to him while Tod had been talking in the café. "I was concerned because he came so close to the time the army will be here. If he was a con man, I wanted to know it before those cavalry troops showed up. More than one of them has been victimized before."

Balder nodded his approval. "Stedman's pretty smart," he said. "If he thinks this Larabee is all right, he most likely is. But it still don't pay for the law to be careless. And this letter can't do no more harm than waste a little time."

He folded the letter and put it into an envelope. He wrote the address with his flourishing hand and rose. "Roper's hired out two of his wagons to go to Boise and bring in supplies and liquor for the big invasion next week," he said. "I can send this down there with one of the drivers and have him bring back the answer."

He nodded good night and left. Cameron realized he was still making a pretense of inspecting his gun and he rammed it back into the holster with a snort. Taking the desk chair, he finished some of the paper work Balder had left and then, when darkness settled in, he rose to make the first of his Saturday night rounds.

On weekends he had to make more trips than at other times and so he moved at a faster pace than he liked. He had found that he gained time by hurrying past those places where there was little chance of trouble — the rear of the hotel and the barber shop and McTigue's Hay and Feed had always been quiet. But the little lane that separated the Hay and Feed from the livery he always inspected carefully. It led from Main Street to the alley and more than once on a Saturday night Cameron had found a drunk from one of the saloons sleeping there out of the wind, an open invitation to someone bent on robbery.

On his left was the fence that separated the alley from McTigue's home. The fence was hedged with roses and where the gate opened onto a graveled pathway leading to McTigue's house, two bushy syringas threw deep shadows onto the alley dirt.

Cameron was almost even with the gate and just short of the lane between the two buildings when he heard the soft click of a

.44 hammer being thumbed back. He stopped and swung his eyes to the left. The sound had come from near the gate, he judged, and now he saw the faint gleam of starlight on gun metal. Someone had his gun barrel resting on the gate top, the muzzle held steadily on Cameron's chest.

Cameron's hand reached automatically for his own gun and then stopped as he realized the futility of this. Before he could begin to clear leather, a bullet could smash him to the ground. He let his hand fall away and stood waiting for the next move.

A dark figure moved out of the lane between the buildings. It was past Cameron, around behind him, before he could turn far enough to the right to make out more than the vaguest shadow. A bootsole scuffed in the alley dirt, and the sound of a heavy object slicing the air filled Cameron's hearing. He tried to throw himself forward, but not quickly enough.

A gun butt drove against the crown of his hat and slid off the side of his head. Pain drove through him in a fiery burst. A second blow caught him on the point of the shoulder. He staggered forward and went to his knees.

The man behind him grunted and caught him by the arms. Cameron was jerked to his feet and held there. He shook his head in an attempt to clear the mist from his eyes, but he could manage only the faintest of blurred outlines. Now the man at the gate opened and shut it and came quickly forward to stop in front of Cameron.

Even through the daze of pain filling his head, Cameron knew what to expect. He had been mousetrapped by one of the oldest tricks — allowing his attention to be turned one way while an assailant came against him from another direction. He had let his guard down after the soft months here and now he was going to pay the price.

While the man behind held him helpless, the man in front was going to whip him. With fists or gun barrel, it didn't matter. As long as the pain gripped him in an icy paralysis, he had no choice but to take his beating.

A fist lashed out, splitting the skin over his cheekbone. His head jerked to the side. Jarring knuckles against his temple snapped him back. The man in front grunted with pleasure and stepped forward. He began cutting at Cameron's face, twisting his knuckles with each blow. The shock cleared Cameron's head and he felt a slight surge of strength through his muscles. At the same time, he found that he could see again.

The man in front was in dark clothing, with a dark handkerchief drawn up to cover him to the eyes. With his hat pulled low over his forehead, he was only a dark bulk in the greater darkness of the alley. But now Cameron could see the movement of his fists and he managed to lean away so that two vicious blows cut air at the side of his head.

The man grunted again, but with less pleasure this time, and drove hard knuckles into Cameron's midriff. Cameron gasped as if he had lost his wind and sagged in the gripping hands holding him from behind. He felt the faintest relaxation of the fingers digging into his biceps, and he surged upward, driving from the knees, throwing himself forward with his head lowered, at the same time twisting his body to wrench his arms free.

The man behind him swore thickly. Cameron's head caught the assailant in front at chest level and forced him back. Cameron kept his legs driving, his torso swinging. His arms came free and he wrapped them around the man giving ground. The one behind clawed wildly at Cameron's back. The three men went into the dust together, Cameron on top of one and under the other.

For a moment he thought he had a chance to work free. But the blood dripping into his eyes blinded him and an elbow slashing against his windpipe cost him the last of his breath. He struggled feebly as he was rolled onto his back and then onto his face and finally pulled again to his feet. He could hear both men panting now, but still neither one spoke.

A boot toe drove out and caught his kneecap, sending a wave of pain and nausea through him. The hands holding his arms let loose and he plunged forward, reaching. Two hands clasped into a single huge fist lashed down against the back of his neck, sending his face toward the thick dust of the alley. As he fell he reached out blindly. His fingers caught cloth, ripped, came loose and he stretched his length in the dirt. He could feel a small bit of the cloth still in his fingers and he clenched his fist, thinking foolishly, flannel, as if he had made an important discovery.

A foot found his ribs, forcing him onto his back. Another foot, boot-heel jabbing, came straight down, grinding into his belly. He felt something give inside and he retched up the last of his wind.

Suddenly a quiet voice from the entrance to the lane between the buildings slipped through the cooling night air, stopping the sounds of the men maneuvering around Cameron. "Leave him alone."

The voice was light, cold, sardonic. "This is a gun I'm holding — so back off. And keep your hands high!"

Still Cameron's assailants said nothing. He could hear their feet carry them away from him and he listened until the sounds faded and there was only thick silence. Then he felt hands, impersonal, neither cruel nor gentle, pull him to his feet. The hands went away and Cameron dropped to his knees.

"Stay there," the man said. "I'll get the kid out of the livery to help you."

He started away and now his voice and the way he moved in the darkness registered on Cameron. This was Sax Larabee.

Sax Larabee had rescued him from a beating that could have meant his death! Why? To put Cameron in his debt? More likely on impulse, Cameron thought, recalling Sax Larabee's unpredictable ways. Another time in the same circumstances he might stand by and watch a man hammered on until he died.

Cameron heard Larabee's bootsoles

whisper over the drying grass in the lane. Then that sound was gone. Time disappeared. He was conscious only of pain and of the necessity to make an effort to keep breathing. Then he became aware of light and noise. Hands touched him and lantern light bit harshly at his eyes.

Tod Purcell swore. "Roy, who did it? Roy . . . ?"

"Get me a bucket of water," Cameron said through battered lips. When the water came, he plunged his head into it. He reared back, snorting, and pulled off his hat. "Dump it over me."

The cold deluge gave him strength enough to get to his feet. With Tod's help, he walked into the livery. He located the horse trough and went head first into it. When he came out, he was able to stand on his feet without help.

"That's a crazy thing to do," Tod said.

"A man knocked me into a cold river once," Cameron said thickly. "He had me beat about as bad as I am now. That water gave me juice enough to climb up the bank and whip him." Surprise crossed his bruised and still bleeding features as his knees gave way and he sat heavily on the edge of the horse trough.

"Or maybe I wasn't beat quite so bad

that other time," he muttered.

"You set still," Tod ordered. "I'll get some help and carry you home."

Cameron had a room at the Widow Crotty's. He thought of the way she would fuss around him, forcibly mother him if he should be bedridden. "No," he said quickly, "help me to the doctor's place. That extra room he calls a hospital is empty right now. I'll stay there tonight and be fine by morning." He forced himself to his feet and started to walk, giving Tod no choice but to come up fast and help him.

"And listen," Cameron said, his voice faint, "when you get back here, take a lantern and go to McTigue's gate. Look around real close. See if you can find anything — the way you found those pricklebush leaves on Larabee's horse. Anything at all that looks out of place by the gate. And then go where you found me in the alley. See if you can locate a little piece of cloth. Flannel I think. I tore it off one of the pair that worked me over."

"All right," Tod said. "Now you shut up. Save your strength for walking."

It was a block and a half to the doctor's house. Cameron remembered only part of the walk. Later Tod told him he moved slower and slower until he was barely going at all when he reached the doctor's porch. Cameron remembered none of that; he recalled only the feel of the splintery wood when he fell on his face at the doctor's front door. After that there was only the darkness, warm and empty of pain.

VI

Tod Purcell had a run of late business at the livery and it was well toward daylight before he had a chance to search the alley.

Footprints and scuffmarks in the alley dirt told plainly where Cameron's two attackers had stood waiting and where the fight had taken place. It was there, between McTigue's fence on the east and the rear of the Hay and Feed on the west, that Tod found the scrap of flannel Cameron had spoken about.

He expected to find little else and he was about to turn away when light from his lantern picked up a bright reflection. Squatting, Tod pushed his finger lightly in the fine dirt. A fleck of gold-colored metal appeared. Another. Then a third.

"Fool's gold!" he breathed in surprise.

He probed further, both in the center of the alley where the fight had taken place and at the sides, where Cameron's attackers had waited. When he left, he had a small mound of the glittering pyrites in his palm. In the livery office, he shook them into one of McTigue's business envelopes. He laid the scrap of flannel on the desk beside the envelope and stared down thoughtfully.

The flannel was plainly a pocket front. It was from a dark red shirt that needed washing badly. And, Tod thought, it shouldn't be too hard to trace. But it was the fool's gold that excited him. He knew there were no pyrites close to town. When he had been younger, he made quite a collection of the mineral, carrying it in a poke the way the miners carried their gold, pretending he had made a big strike.

He recalled now that the only two good sources for fool's gold were the mines on the benchland back of Cameron's spread, and some long abandoned tunnels up in the high-mountain country that blocked off the south end of the valley. And the finest place of all had been that mine in the box canyon a short way up from Rafe Arker's place — the one where the Dondee brothers were working now.

Fool's gold and pricklebush leaves — both from the hill country where Rafe Arker and the Dondees lived! And just as the pricklebush leaves had attached themselves to a horse, so could the fool's gold have worked into men's boots and dropped off there in the alley.

Not Rafe, Tod decided. He had seen Joe Farley pack the big man into a buckboard and haul him home as much dead as alive that night of his fight with Cameron. The Dondees then? He shook his head. He knew too little about them to say. Come daylight, he'd get the flannel and the envelope to Cameron and let him decide what they meant.

The day man showed up late, and by the time Tod got to Doctor Draper's house, the town was beginning to stir with life. His knock brought the doctor himself to the door.

"I got to see Roy," Tod said earnestly. "It's real important."

"Come back about this time tomorrow," the doctor said. "He might be awake by then." He frowned. "The rap on the head he took hurt him worse than I thought last night."

His words jolted Tod. Somehow he had come to think of Roy Cameron as indestructible. He walked slowly away, trying to understand what this meant. He was crossing the main street, going toward Jenny's café, when he saw Sax Larabee step from the hotel lobby and stroll south toward the livery barn. "Business on Sunday too?" he thought wonderingly. Stopping, he watched Larabee.

Larabee disappeared into the livery barn. Moments later he appeared on the bay horse he had come to favor. He walked the horse slowly south.

Tod hurried into the café to find Jenny getting ready for the morning customers. She served him pie and coffee and while he gulped it down, he told her what he had learned.

"The doctor said Roy would be all right in a few days — a few days!" Jenny exclaimed. "Why should anyone beat him so badly? And especially those Dondee brothers — if they were the ones."

Tod showed her the pyrites. "It sure looks like they was the ones in the alley." He frowned. "That stranger, Larabee, was there too — lucky for Roy. But I sure don't trust him much more'n I do the Dondees. He went riding south this morning again. I'd like to know why he always goes to the same place if he's so interested in looking at mining properties."

"There are lots of mines on the bench," Jenny pointed out.

"There ain't many places where pricklebush leaves grow," Tod argued. "And every time Larabee comes back, he brings some with him." He stopped eating and talking long enough to scribble a note on a leaf from Jenny's account pad. He put the pyrites and the flannel and the note in the envelope and pushed it across the counter. "I'm going to ride after that Larabee right now and see where he goes," he said. "If Roy comes to before I get back, give him these and tell him what I said."

"I don't think . . ." Jenny began, and stopped. Tod's expression told her that nothing she could say would change his plans. She turned away and began to wrap some food for him.

"Just be careful, Tod. If the Dondees did ambush Roy last night, they're nobody to fool with. And remember that Rafe lives down that way." She thrust a package of bread and cold beef toward him. "Even if it means being late to work tonight, you come here as soon as you get back!"

"Roy taught me how to track," Tod said. "I won't get in no trouble." He slid off the stool. "But I won't be coming back. I fixed it with McTigue so I can start working for Obed tomorrow. Unless I find out something Roy ought to know right away, I'll ride on west."

Taking the food, he hurried out. Larabee would be well down the valley now, but Tod wasn't concerned. He was sure he knew where the man was heading and that he could find him quickly enough. At the livery, he saddled his paint pony, stored the food in his saddle bags, added a canteen of water, and slipped his varmint rifle into the boot.

He took his time on the trail, letting the paint warm up well before he let it run. He slowed the horse before topping each rise, not wanting to warn Larabee by running onto him. But he was almost to Cameron's spread before he had a glimpse of the bay and its rider. And that, he thought, was pure luck. The valley floor was empty ahead of him except for a few grazing cattle. But when Tod looked east from a high spot, he saw Larabee working his way along the ridge that ran behind the timber sweeping up from the valley floor.

Tod frowned, wondering why Larabee would ride a hard trail when he could take an easy one. It was a lot shorter way from town onto the bench, but because of the deadfalls and the washed-out bridges over the creeks, it made for hard riding. It could save time, all right, if a man was in a hurry. But from what he could see, Larabee was picking his way along like he was out for a Sunday ride.

Riding the ridge trail was one way to cut down the risk of being seen, of course. But who would Larabee be hiding from? The very fact of the man taking so many pains increased Tod's suspicion. And now to protect himself, he rode closer to the edge of the timber, out of Larabee's sight.

Larabee could only be riding for Arker's place or the Dondees' mine, Tod was sure. And so after a short ride south, he angled eastward into the timber, following a short cut that would bring him onto the wagonroad before Larabee reached it. When he reached the south edge of the trees, he stopped, looking carefully up the road. The rutted trail leading to Arker's place was almost directly across from him. The side trail that led into the Dondees' box canyon was visible at the top of a curve in the road well upslope. It was here that Tod fixed his attention.

He heard Larabee coming and then, shortly, saw him ride into view. But instead of reining the bay toward the Dondees' place, he came on down the road and swung toward Rafe Arker's. Tod waited until he was swallowed by the cut and then he spurred the paint forward. Pulling up in the pine thicket, he turned the horse off the trail and tied it. Then he moved forward on foot, following a narrow track that went over the east side of the hill through which the cut ran. He dropped down on the far side where the hill tapered into Arker's yard, a little distance behind the blank rear wall of his cabin.

Tod moved quietly now, easing along the way Cameron had taught him until he was pressed against the cabin wall. He located a spot where the mud chinking had dropped from between the logs and tried to see inside. The narrow space between the two logs wasn't enough for him to see anything but by listening closely he could hear most of what was being said inside.

He was in time to hear Arker's rumble: "I don't know who whipped Cameron, but it wasn't me and Joe. I ain't in shape yet to fight a rabbit. But I'll be ready in a couple days and then that lawman better watch out."

"Don't be a fool," Larabee's cold voice snapped. "I told you most people in town think you beat up Cameron last night. If anything happens to him when you're on your feet, they'll come after you with a posse. And I want you free to move around Saturday night."

Free for what, Tod wondered. He heard Larabee add: "Do it my way and you'll end up getting everything you want — Cameron, money, and that Purcell woman." The door slammed, and in a moment Tod heard the jangle of harness as Larabee rode away.

"That Larabee's smart, Rafe," Joe Farley said. "You do like he says."

Rafe Arker laughed. "If it gets me all them things, I sure will." The laughter faded from his voice. "Especially that lawman. He's what I want the most."

Tod hurried back the way he had come, not wanting to risk losing Larabee now. He guessed the man would go to the Dondees' place, but he had thought that before and been wrong.

When he reached the top of the hill, he glimpsed Larabee turning upslope on the wagonroad. He hurried down to the paint and climbed into the saddle. As eager as he was, he forced himself to walk the horse so as to give Larabee time to get out of sight. Even so, when he reached the road, Larabee was just turning onto the trail that led to the box canyon. He disappeared around a shoulder of rock, and Tod spurred the paint.

Where the trail led into the box canyon, Tod reined in and dropped to the ground. He tied the paint behind the shoulder of rock, out of sight, and moved forward on foot again. But now he could feel the weariness that came from more than twenty hours without sleep tugging at him. As excited as he was, the warming sun made his eyes heavy, his movements slow. He swallowed a yawn as he stopped just before the trail broke around the rock shoulder and into the box canyon.

Pressing himself to the rock, he blinked his eyes to clear them and leaned forward, peering into the canyon. He could see Larabee and Jupe Dondee standing in the middle of the clearing. They seemed to be arguing about something but he was too far away to catch more than an occasional word. But from the way Jupe was glaring at a small mound of glittering pyrites on the ground at his feet, Tod guessed the argument was about that. Then Hale Dondee came down the steep trail from the mine dug into the hillside. He had a good-sized sack in his hand and he waved it at Larabee.

"I guess you outfoxed yourself, Larabee, when you said we could keep anything we made mining. Look at this!" His voice was excited, loud enough for Tod to hear him clearly. Tod swallowed back a desire to laugh when Jupe took the sack and up-ended it, sending a glittering stream of pyrites onto the pile at his feet. He said something the boy failed to catch and Hale began to stomp around, swearing. When he calmed down, he spoke to Larabee.

Tod caught only an occasional word: ". . . Saturday night . . . lawman . . ."

A light puff of breeze down the canyon wall carried most of Larabee's words to Tod, but they made little sense: "Cameron . . . you gave him more of a beating than I wanted. . . . We'll be lucky if he's up and around by Saturday." And after Jupe said something in a lower voice, ". . . I want him alive and on his feet when we make the hit."

Tod was still trying to put meaning to Larabee's words when the three men moved toward the cabin set on the far side of the small canyon. He frowned in disappointment. To reach the cabin, he would have to cross better than twenty yards of open ground, most of it in view of the two front windows. But now that he knew the Dondees were the ones who had ambushed Cameron, he felt he had to take the risk and learn what was going on.

He stayed as close to the rock wall of the canyon as he could, easing along with his gaze fixed on the cabin, ready to turn and bolt if the door should come open. He wished he had a gun but the only one he owned was back with the paint.

The twenty yards were covered with agonizing slowness, but finally he reached a point even with the corner of the cabin. Breathing easier, he turned and sprinted to his right. He reached the cabin wall and dropped to his knees until he caught his breath. Then he sought a weak spot where he might overhear as he had at Rafe Arker's place. But this cabin was too tightly built and finally he risked crawling around beneath one of the open front windows.

Shock ran through him as he heard Larabee's smooth, cold voice saying, "I want Cameron there because when the time comes for us to make our play, he's the one man who won't interfere."

And Hale Dondee said, "You trying to tell me that Cameron'll let us bust open that bank?"

A horse neighing from the corral behind the building drowned out the rest of Hale's words. When the sound quieted, Tod heard Larabee say, "When the time comes, he'll be looking the other way."

Not Roy, Tod thought desperately. He couldn't be in with these men. He couldn't be part of a plan to rob the bank of the money paid in by the army! But then, why had the Dondees beaten him up? Had he been part of the plan and then tried to back out — and given a beating to bring him back into line?

Then he heard Jupe Dondee say, "If he don't run scared? Or if he don't do things the way you want him to — what then?"

Larabee's answer came so softly that Tod barely heard it. "He will. That's my job — to see that he does nothing while we help ourselves to over twenty thousand dollars worth of gold."

To see that Roy did nothing while . . . Tod sucked in his breath. Some way, Larabee had a hold on Roy Cameron. Some way, he was going to force Roy to help him steal the money that was going to help the valley people get through the long winter ahead. He had to help, he thought. He had to find Roy and get him to explain so he could know what to do to help.

The sound of footsteps coming toward the front door brought Tod to his feet. Panic surged through him and he turned and bolted across the open yard. Behind him a voice shouted in surprise and anger. Before he was halfway to the protection of the shoulder of rock a gun blasted. Lead tugged at Tod's hat, and he flung himself forward in a weaving run in a desperate effort to cover the last twenty feet of open ground.

"It's that kid from the livery!" Jupe Dondee bellowed.

"He's thick with Cameron," Larabee snapped. "God knows how much he heard. Don't let him get back to town. Shoot him!"

Another bullet whispered angrily as it came close to Tod. Then he was behind the rock shoulder and momentarily safe. But not for long, he knew. Larabee's horse was handy. He would be aboard and coming fast enough. Gasping now, Tod ran to where the paint waited.

He jerked the reins free and flung himself into the saddle. He barely had the pony headed downslope when Larabee burst out of the canyon entrance. Tod spurred the paint but he knew that in open pursuit, Larabee's bay could run him down. He had ridden the horse himself more than once. It was fast and tough. Frantically he looked around for help. The protection of the timbered slope rising up from the valley beckoned. But he rejected the idea. Once in there, the three men could bottle him up. Nor did he dare try to reach the valley floor. He would be ridden down before he could get to it.

Now he was past the top of the timber, the paint flying as it raced downhill. The rutted track leading to Arker's place appeared on

Tod's left. But there was no safety there — Arker was Larabee's man. Not at Arker's, but what of the hills beyond his shack? That was country Tod knew, country that Larabee and the Dondee brothers could not know. Once in those hills he could work into the high country. If he could lose them even for a short time, he could cut west, across the stagecoach road leading out of the valley and on to Obed Begg's place. And of all the men he could think of, Obed would be the best one to turn to for help.

Three guns opened up behind him. He glanced back to see that the Dondees had joined Larabee. He reined the paint sharply to his left, putting it on the rutted track. Rifle bullets kicked dirt near the pony's feet. But the maneuver had surprised his pursuers, had given him a little precious time.

He pressed the paint grimly. If Rafe and Farley weren't waiting at the other side of the cut, he would have a chance for safety. But the sounds of shooting were almost sure to bring them out of the shack.

Even so, he had no choice. He could only spur the paint on.

VII

It was still fairly quiet in Cougar Hill when Sax Larabee rode the little rented bay south from the livery barn. He was a man careful with animals and he made the horse go slowly until its muscles were loose. Then he turned from the stagecoach road and worked his way onto the ridge that would take him south.

An observant man, he had learned a good deal about the lay of the Cougar country since coming here, and if he had wished, he could have made a quick trip to the mining country. But he preferred to ride slowly and avoid being seen. Even so, he caught a glimpse of a rider down on the valley floor who acted as if he might be looking up at the ridge. Then he recognized Tod Purcell, and decided the boy was probably just out checking Cameron's cattle for him.

Once on the wagonroad, Larabee dropped downslope to Arker's trail and rode on through the cut to the small stump ranch cupped by logged-off hills. Larabee shook his head as he looked around. He found it hard to understand how men could live the way Arker and Farley did.

The cabin was a sag-roofed affair of badly chinked logs and with window panes of scraped gut instead of proper glass. The outbuildings had a desolate, half ruined look about them. The corral was weed-grown, and scum clung to the edges of the horse trough. Inside, he found the cabin's one room in as poor shape as the outdoors. The stove was stained with cooked food, and dirty dishes were scattered over the lone table. Arker and Farley sat on back-less chairs, sucking coffee noisily from broken-handled mugs.

Arker grunted and talked carefully through his still swollen mouth. "Coffee pot's on the stove."

Larabee made an effort to hide his disgust at the stench in the place. He lit a cheroot and wrapped himself in its smoke and thought bitterly of what a man had to put up with to satisfy his passion for revenge. And it seemed perfectly logical to his mind that the blame for his having to deal with a man like Rafe Arker belonged to Cameron.

Larabee said, "I didn't come here to drink coffee. I came to tell you to watch for the law."

Arker snorted. "There ain't no law outside the town limits — unless you count the sheriff over at the county seat. And he ain't about to bother me, not when he has to ride a hundred miles across these mountains." He glared at Larabee and added, "What the devil would the law want with me now?"

"Two men jumped Cameron in the east alley last night and put him in the hospital," Larabee said.

"And he claims it was me, I suppose," Arker grunted.

"Cameron's in no shape to talk," Larabee answered. "But I broke up the fight and I can swear it wasn't you two."

"Who did it?" Arker demanded.

"It was too dark for me to tell," Larabee lied. "I thought you might have hired somebody. The town thinks it was you, naturally."

"I don't know who whipped Cameron," Arker insisted. "But it wasn't me and Joe. I ain't in shape yet to fight a rabbit. But I'll be ready in a couple days and then that lawman better watch out."

"Don't be a fool," Larabee snapped. "I told you most people in town think you beat up Cameron last night. If anything happens to him when you're on your feet, they'll come after you with a posse. And I want you free to move around Saturday night."

He blew a cloud of smoke. "Do it my way and you'll end up getting everything you want — Cameron, money, and that Purcell woman."

He waited no longer but turned to go. He could stand just so much of Rafe Arker and the filth that he lived in. Whatever Arker had for an answer was lost in the sound of the slamming door.

He breathed deeply, gratefully, of the fresh air as he rode the bay slowly through the cut. He wished he didn't have to deal with a man like Arker. He couldn't be trusted to follow orders as they had to be followed if this plan was to be a success. And, he knew, Arker resented him — his easy way of handling problems, his brains. Knowing this, he had plans to take care of Arker if it should become necessary.

Larabee always planned to take care of every contingency. He had been meticulous in his planning ever since that one time he had failed to do so — and had spent three years of his life in a prison cell.

Those same three years had developed in him his one great weakness — his overriding desire for revenge on Roy Cameron.

At times the force of his hatred for Cameron frightened him. He had tried many times to cleanse his mind of this by trying to accept Cameron's story about the bank robbery. But the facts as Larabee saw them added up to only one answer — Cameron had doublecrossed him.

During his time in prison he read through the warden's library. And because the warden had once been a mining lawyer, Larabee came to know a great deal about the subject. After his release, he put his knowledge to work — he acquired properties cheaply and sold them at large profits. He made a good deal of money over the years, and he spent it — buying a home in San Francisco, buying land of speculation with long term profits in mind, and buying information about Roy Cameron.

At one time Larabee had four Pinkerton men working for him. And slowly he built up a picture of Cameron during the long, hate-filled years. More than once he was tempted to appear where Cameron worked and denounce him as a criminal masquerading as a lawman. But each time he curbed himself, knowing that in most western towns such a background would not be to Cameron's disfavor. Too many lawmen had ridden the wild trails. But finally

Cameron settled in Cougar Hill, and Larabee knew that here the temper of the people was different. Here, Cameron could be hurt.

And then, as if to mock all of Larabee's efforts, his investments began to fail. His money disappeared. He mortgaged his home, sold his properties, and he found himself without the capital he needed to work the one big deal he hoped would make him a truly rich man.

The report he had received from the Pinkerton man who found Cameron in the Cougar valley country told Larabee a good deal about the town itself. And as he read it, he realized he might have found the way to finally revenge himself for those three years in prison and at the same time get the capital he needed. By train and then by stage, he worked his way to Idaho Territory. Here he learned all he could about Cougar Hill and the valley. He hired the Dondee brothers, men he had used before, and sent them ahead of him. He heard about Rafe and waited patiently for him to be released from prison.

Thinking about Arker made Larabee smile with satisfaction. He had handled the man perfectly. As far is Arker knew, their meeting a half day's ride from the prison had been lucky coincidence. And Arker would go on thinking this, never realizing that he was being used. Or not realizing it until nothing he could do would change the inevitable. The fact that Arker would be destroyed did not bother Larabee. He despised men of Arker's type. In his opinion, the world would be better off without them.

As he rode up the wagonroad to the benchland, Larabee thought of how easily he could have destroyed Roy Cameron. He could have killed him last night. Or he could have stood by and let him be killed. But that would not have been enough. Cameron had to know the pain of loneliness, of being without friends. He had to know the humiliation of defeat. And above all, he had to live long enough to know who had brought him the pain, the humiliation, the defeat.

A narrow trail led Larabee from the wagonroad into a box canyon. Here the Dondees had their shack and their mine. Fresh dirt scattered on a pile of weed grown tailings testified that they were actually working. Larabee was pleased and surprised to see this. He was more surprised to hear sounds of a pick and shovel coming from the large hole that was the entrance to the old mine the Dondees had taken over.

He whistled shrilly and in a few moments Jupe Dondee appeared. He tossed down the shovel he was carrying and hurried down the path to where Larabee waited.

"This is Sunday," Larabee said. "You don't have to overdo the business of being a miner."

Jupe Dondee grinned behind his straggle of beard. "Hell," he said, "look at this!" He pulled a poke from his pocket and opened it. He shook glittering flakes into the palm of his hand. "Look!"

Larabee looked. He took the poke and upended it, letting a glittering stream fall to the ground. "What the hell you think you're doing? That's a week's hard work!" Jupe cried angrily.

"These are iron pyrites," Larabee said disgustedly. "Fool's gold. Your week's work is worth less than that poke. Now stop wasting my time and call Hale down here. We've got business to take care of."

Jupe Dondee stared from the mineral in his palm to the pile on the ground. He lifted his head and carefully studied Larabee's expression. His suspicion was obvious, but after a moment it faded reluctantly away.

He emptied his palm and brushed his hands. "I guess you ought to know," he said grudgingly. Turning aside, he shouted for his brother.

Hale Dondee came out of the hole and down the short, steep trail. He was carrying a good-sized sack and showing his broken teeth in a wide grin. "I guess you outfoxed yourself, Larabee, when you said we could keep anything we made mining. Look at this!" He slapped the sack with his free hand.

Jupe Dondee grabbed the sack from his brother and upended it, spilling the glittering pyrites onto the pile. "Larabee says this is fool's gold," he grunted. "It ain't worth as much as the dirt it's laying on."

Hale swore loudly. He stomped around, accusing Larabee of trying to cheat them. But after a time, he calmed down and shrugged philosophically.

"There'll be plenty of the real stuff come Saturday night," he said finally. He laughed. "How's the lawman today? You think he'll bother us when we make our hit?"

"Cameron won't bother us," Larabee assured him. He frowned. "But you gave him more of a beating than I wanted. If I hadn't stopped you when I did, he'd be in that hospital for a month. As it is, we'll be lucky if he's up and around by Saturday."

Jupe stared at him in open amazement. "Lucky! You gone crazy? What do you want the law up and around for?"

Larabee turned on him savagely. "I know what I'm doing. I told you before that I want him alive and on his feet when we make the hit."

Jupe rubbed his knuckles. "That still don't make no sense to me. Cameron's a wildcat. The next time I tangle with him, I want an army behind me and a gun in my hand."

Larabee started for the small shack. "Make me some coffee and I'll try to get the idea through your head."

Inside, the cabin's one room was fairly neat. At least, Larabee thought, it didn't stink like Rafe Arker's place. He dropped onto one of the two chairs and stretched his booted feet in front of him. "Here's the plan," he said. "Get it clear and don't try to change it. The army will be here at the end of the week. They'll look over the stock Beggs and his crews are bringing down from the hills and buy what they want. From what I hear, they're hungry for horses and mules and the ranchers have some good stock for them. That means there'll be even more money than I thought at first. Stedman, that banker, estimated between eighty and a hundred thousand dollars all told."

"That's a lot of gold," Hale Dondee breathed.

"And it's all ours if we play things right," Larabee answered. "The way they work things here is for this Obed Beggs to take charge of everything. The army pays him every man's share. He puts the money in the bank as it comes to him. Most of it will be there by late Friday with the last dribbles in on Saturday morning. By Saturday afternoon the last of the army will be gone with the stock. The bank is locked up and the ranchers go about their regular business until Monday. Then they come to town and Beggs parcels out the shares, including the wages for the townsmen and such people."

Jupe Dondee finished lighting a fire in the cook stove and set the coffee pan on the hottest part of the rusty surface. "So most of the gold will be in the bank by Friday night and all of it by Saturday afternoon — waiting for us."

"There'll be more money than this Cougar country ever saw at one time," Larabee said. "And you can be sure that the law will have its eye on that bank."

"But you said . . ." Jupe started to protest.

"I said I wanted Cameron up and around — and guarding the bank Saturday night," Larabee snapped. "I don't want Balder or some valley rancher nervous enough to shoot at shadows. I want Cameron there because when the time comes for us to make our play, he's the one man who won't interfere."

Both men gaped at him. Hale Dondee snorted loudly. "You trying to tell me Cameron'll let us bust open that bank? Not him, Larabee. I watched him operate long enough to know that he won't help us if we was to give him all the gold and the bank building too. You got the wrong man, thinking that Cameron'll . . ."

"I know what I'm doing," Larabee retorted. "I said Cameron won't bother us, and he won't. When the time comes, he'll be looking the other way."

He smiled coldly. "And I intend to fix things so that Balder and the rest of the town's big men will be spending their time accusing Cameron of having helped in the robbery instead of going after us. They're either going to think that Cameron was part of the gang or that his beating made him run scared."

"And if he don't run scared?" Jupe Dondee demanded. "Or if he don't do things the way you want him to — what then?"

"He will," Larabee said softly. "That's my job — to see that he does nothing while we help ourselves to over eighty thousand dollars worth of gold."

VIII

It was Tuesday night before Cameron realized he was alive. Before that his mind held only vague blurs of memory. He recalled the ambush, the coming of Sax Larabee, and Tod's helping him to the doctor's house. After that there was mostly darkness, with now and then a faint bit of light — remembrance of Balder, of Obed Beggs, of Sax Larabee, and especially of Jenny Purcell. But there was no recall of Tod at all, and Cameron lay wondering at this.

He rolled his head on the pillow as the door to his room came open. The spare figure of Doctor Draper appeared. "Ah, I hoped you'd come awake tonight," he said. "How's the appetite?"

"I have one," Cameron said dryly. "My stomach feels like it missed Sunday dinner."

"And a few more meals," the doctor agreed. "This is Tuesday, Roy."

Surprise brought Cameron sitting up. Pain lanced at his ribs and into his right shoulder. He fell back.

106

"You'll need a while yet before you can get up and around," the doctor said. "You got a nasty crack on the head and some badly bruised ribs."

Cameron lay back, his eyes closed, and tried to comprehend that he had lost three days out of his life. He thought of the roundup and grunted. Both Obed and Balder could have used him those three days.

And then his mind turned to Sax Larabee and cold shadows of trouble clouded him. The memory of Sax appearing in the alley rescuing him brought the shadows into harsh focus. There was something wrong with that scene, something Cameron felt he should be able to put words to. But his mind was too tired, and he felt Sax Larabee drift out of it.

The doctor appeared with chicken soup. He said, "Jenny made it for you. She's on the roundup most of the time, but she said to tell you she'd be back by Friday at the latest." He added as if this needed explaining, "I assured her you were all right; otherwise she would have spent all her time right here."

"I guessed as much," Cameron said. He sat up, carefully this time. "By the time she gets here, I should be ready to ride."

"By next month, maybe," the doctor

said. "You try moving too soon and you'll be back in bed — for a long stretch."

Cameron said nothing but started eating. When he was through and Draper had taken the empty soup bowl away, he threw back the covers and tried standing up. He moved too quickly at first and dizziness forced him back to the bed. But after a time he managed to stay on his feet for five and then ten minutes at a time. Satisfied, he turned down the lamp and went to sleep.

It was late on Wednesday before he had a chance to test his legs again. Balder came in the morning to talk about the ambush. Cameron had little to offer and Balder nothing.

"I asked Tod to look around for me," Cameron said. "But he hasn't shown up."

"He left for the roundup Sunday," Balder said. He obviously didn't consider anything Tod might have to say worth much in the way of help. "I figure it was Rafe and Farley. So do most folks. But that Larabee who busted up the fight claims neither one of the pair was big enough for Rafe. Besides, I hear he's been in bed mostly since last Thursday night. If it wasn't Rafe, who was it? Who else had any reason to jump you that way?"

This question was one Cameron had spent a good many hours turning over in his mind. He felt sure he had part of the answer — but not enough of it to make any real sense yet.

He said, "Right now I'm worried about Tod. When he says he'll do something for me, he usually does it."

"Obed Beggs'll be in for grub later today or early tomorrow. I'll ask him about the kid," Balder said. He had little more to say except to relieve Cameron's worries about the law work, remarking that the army men had arrived and set some of their own troops to patrol themselves.

He hadn't been gone long when Obed Beggs wandered in, grinning his pleasure at seeing Cameron sitting up and wide awake. "The work's going better'n I expected," he told Cameron. "So there's no need for you to fret yourself about helping out. Just do what Doc Draper says and stay put in this bed."

His grin widened. "Besides, Jenny's doing enough work for the both of you. She knows the high country better'n anybody in these parts, so we've got all but a couple of mountain meadows cleaned out. It looks like we'll have most everything corralled and turned over to the army by Saturday noon."

"Tod knows the high country pretty well too," Cameron said. "Between him and Jenny, everything in it should be cleaned out."

Obed snorted. "That kid. I don't know what's got into him. He was supposed to drift in Sunday night, but I ain't seen nor heard a thing. I don't know where he's got himself to."

Up to now Cameron's concern for Tod had been a mild thing, built mostly on surprise that the boy hadn't come to tell him what he'd found in the alley. But as the meaning of Obed's words sank in, Cameron felt a cold finger of fear touch him. What if Tod had found something that pointed to the ambushers? He would have come here, of course: But then he would have been told Cameron was still unconscious. And Cameron knew with frightening certainty exactly what Tod would do in such a case. Wanting to make Cameron proud of him — and perhaps to revenge the beating — he would go after the ambushers himself.

Cameron tried to brush aside the shadows in his mind. He was guessing, imagining too much. Tod just as well could have attached himself to one of the small crews working far in the hills, having forgotten in his excitement at working the roundup all about his obligation to report to Obed Beggs.

After Obed left, Cameron lay for some time arguing with himself. Finally he stood up and walked out of the room to find the doctor. He moved slowly but steadily, pleased to discover that he was no longer dizzy when he got out of bed.

Doctor Draper cursed him pleasantly and ran him back to bed. "Don't try to be so tough," he said.

"I wasn't trying to prove anything," Cameron said. "I wanted to know if you'd seen Tod Purcell since Saturday night?"

"He was here early Sunday morning," the doctor answered. "Now lie still and let me have a look at those ribs."

Cameron obliged. He said, "Did he say anything when he was here?"

"He asked for you. That's all. No — he said it was important for him to see you."

The sharp pains from the doctor's probing fingers went almost unnoticed. Tod had found something and he had come to report it. Cameron's impulse was to get up and out of there, to find Tod if he could. But the short walk he had taken left him more tired than he expected. His muscles felt soggy. To try to do anything

111

now — if there was anything left to do after four days — would help no one.

Doctor Draper straightened up. "Don't try any fast draws for a while, Roy. Move your right arm too fast and the pain will hit you like another kick in the ribs."

"All right," Cameron said.

By Friday morning he was feeling comparatively fit again, and he was walking around when Jenny came shortly before dinnertime. She wore her work clothes and had obviously just come off the roundup. Her smile warmed Cameron as she came eagerly forward to kiss him. Then she led him firmly back to the bed.

"Doctor Draper warned me you'd try to show off by staying up," she said.

Cameron lay back. "How's the work going?"

"Everything's in on the eastern end of the mountains but the high pockets," she said. "Obed and his crews are cleaning out the west country. Tomorrow I'll go up to Rainy Creek meadows and that'll be the end of it."

Cameron recalled her having taken him twice into the high mountains just east of the south pass. He said, "Keep an eye out this time of year. Cold or even a snow could catch you up there."

"I'll ride up in the morning and have the stock down before afternoon," Jenny said. She sat on the edge of the bed, and now he caught the glint of worry in her eyes.

"You're thinking about Tod," he said.

"Have you heard . . ." She broke off, shaking her head. "Of course you wouldn't have. I'm jumping at straws."

He said with sudden knowledge, "You have a pretty good idea where he went."

Jenny hesitated, but finally she nodded.

"He told you something before he left town?" Cameron queried.

Reluctantly, Jenny unbuttoned her shirt pocket and drew out a crumpled envelope. "Sunday, Tod gave me this to pass on to you. I didn't give it to you before because I didn't want you to have this to worry about — not until you're on your feet again. But it's been so long without a word!"

Cameron took the envelope and opened it. He slipped Tod's brief note out and stared down at the parcel of flannel and at the bit of fool's gold. He read the note carefully.

"He went to the Dondees to see what he could find out," Cameron guessed.

"I think so," Jenny answered. "I've been meaning to ride that way, but I've been so busy and then the most probable answer is that Tod is with one of the small crews that went deep in the hills."

Cameron could see worry and weariness battling hard within her. He said gently, "You go get some rest. Tod's pretty good at taking care of himself, and he most likely is somewhere in the hills with Obed's men."

"The stableman told me that Tod rode out on that little paint pony he likes so well — the one with the funny frog in the left hind hoof. It leaves a little forked mark in the dirt." She shook her head as she rose to leave. "Can Tod be right? Why would the Dondees want to beat you that way?"

"I don't know it was them," Cameron said. "Tod was just guessing. They can't have had any reason that I know of."

As he spoke an idea burst in his mind. Quickly, he thrust it away until Jenny left. After she went, promising to rest up for the rough ride she would have tomorrow, he lay and examined his idea. He knew now what had bothered him about Sax Larabee appearing in the alley — it wasn't like Sax to poke his nose in other men's business; and it wasn't like him to go out of his way to help a man he hated as much as he obviously hated Cameron.

"Sax hired that pair to jump me!" Cameron thought. Knowing Larabee as he did, Cameron thought it was possible Larabee had gone so far as to send the brothers here ahead of himself — to get a feel for the Cougar country and the kind of people in it through what they could tell him.

More and more, Cameron realized how dangerous Sax Larabee really was. And again he felt the bite of the cold, thin fear at the thought of Larabee's quick, calculating brain, at his complete ruthless disregard for anyone, for anything but the goal he set for himself.

If Tod had gone to the Dondees' mine and found Larabee there with the brothers, and if Larabee had caught him . . .

Cameron waited no longer. He rose and dressed, moving carefully to husband his strength. He found his gun and belt in the wardrobe, hanging on a hook under his hat. He winced at the darts of pain that came each time he moved his right arm a little too fast or lifted it a little too high. But his strength was still holding up when he was ready to leave, and for this he was grateful.

He slipped out through the window, not wanting to take the time to argue with Doctor Draper. By the time he was discovered missing, he hoped to be well into the valley, well on his way to the Dondees' mine.

IX

Cameron rode slowly, letting the roan warm its muscles and getting himself accustomed to the saddle. After a time, he stepped up the pace until they were going at a smooth, ground-eating lope. Cameron was pleased to find that except for an occasional stabbing pain across his ribs he could handle himself well enough.

He dropped the roan's speed as he reached his own land. It looked as if nothing had been disturbed — the small bunch of cattle grazed peacefully on the thick grass at the bottom edge of the timbered slope, two cows drifted toward the spring a short distance ahead, and a young bull was romping around the edge of the herd as if he hoped to get into trouble. Cameron made a quick count and decided that Rafe Arker hadn't been back for a second helping of beef.

Cutting across the grass to the wagonroad, Cameron started up to the bench. When he came to the softer dirt, he stopped to look for any sign that might be worth reading. He found nothing until he reached the beginning of Rafe Arker's road. He grunted softly. There had been a good deal of traffic along Arker's trail a few days back, but for the moment Cameron's interest was in only one set of prints — those belonging to Tod's little paint. He located the fork mark he sought and examined it closely. He judged that it had been made Sunday or, at the latest, Monday. Other prints overlaid it, and they looked to be about the same age.

Cameron rode uproad a short distance and stopped again. Here the prints left by the paint were clearer, easier to read. Tod had ridden toward the bench at a fairly slow pace, but he had been pushing his pony coming back down. From the way the soft dirt had spurted, fuzzing the edge of the sign, Cameron read this piece of Tod's story easily enough.

Tod had followed someone up toward the bench — a single rider, a man but not too heavy a one. But coming down he had been the one followed — and three different horsemen had been close on his heels.

On impulse, Cameron swung the roan and rode back to Arker's trail. He followed it slowly, now and then picking up a hoofprint where the weedy grass failed to grow. Tod had been chased along here too, he saw. Then Cameron picked up a second set of the paint's prints and frowned, puzzled. He was too old a hand at reading sign to mistrust his own judgment, yet these hoofmarks seemed to say that Tod had ridden this trail three times within a short while — he had gone in slowly and come out only a little faster, and then he had gone in again riding like a cougar was after him.

Cameron could pretty well guess who the boy's pursuers were — the Dondees and either Joe Farley or Sax Larabee. Not Rafe Arker. No horse carrying his weight had been along this stretch of trail for some time. If it was Farley, then that meant Rafe had teamed up with the Dondees. It wasn't a prospect Cameron liked. Each outfit would be hard enough to handle alone, without their working together under Sax Larabee.

Cameron rode very slowly now, reading the story left in the soft dirt. He saw where Tod had pulled off the trail and tied his pony to a scrub pine. He spotted the bootprints that told him Tod had climbed the shoulder of the cut, going toward Rafe Arker's cabin. And he was able to tell that

Tod had come running back to the horse — not wildly like a man in panic, but quick and easy.

He followed someone into Rafe's and then out again, Cameron guessed. But on his second trip in, Tod had pushed the paint right on into the cut, still driving it at top speed, and still being followed by three riders pressing close.

Cameron started to pull his carbine free of the boot but the pain jabbed up through his right side and he lost his grip on the gun butt. Swearing, he reached across with his left hand and brought the carbine up. He laid it across his lap and then turned the roan into the cut. As he came out into bright sunlight at the far end, he pulled up. Two horses were tied at the railing before the door of Arker's ramshackle cabin. One was saddled; the other was loaded with a well-lashed pack. Cameron could see no other signs of life — the weed-grown corral stood empty; nothing stirred around the barn; no smoke came from the tired chimney of the house.

Cameron rode forward, picking up the paint's trail. It went straight ahead, cutting across Arker's yard toward the hills behind the sag-fenced corral. Cameron rode that way but he lost the sign on the rocky hillside.

"You there!"

It was Rafe Arker's heavy voice. Cameron turned the roan just far enough to put the muzzle of the carbine on the cabin door. Rafe Arker stood there, half in and half out of the doorway. He held his .44 in one hand, a glass of murky looking beer incongruously in the other.

"Cameron, by God!" Surprise rode Arker's voice.

"What's the matter, Arker," Cameron mocked, "didn't you expect to see me up and around yet?"

Arker took a belligerent step forward. "What's that supposed to mean?"

Cameron studied him thoughtfully. Arker was close enough so that the signs of last week's fight showed plainly on his face. But he looked strong — strong enough to have been up and around for some time now. And Tod could have been wrong about the Dondees. Rafe Arker was the logical man to have ambushed him. Sax Larabee's testimony was not likely to have much meaning. His claim that neither man was big enough to be Rafe Arker could be just so many empty words.

Cameron said now, "Saturday night I was whipsawed and beaten up. A lot of people think it was your kind of trick."

"Saturday night I was still in bed," Arker

rumbled. "I didn't get on my feet until Tuesday, and I didn't do no roundup work until yesterday." He waved his beer glass at the two horses. "I ain't much good yet for riding down wild stuff so they sent me back for supplies."

That the man would offer any kind of explanation surprised Cameron. That he would offer more explanation than he needed to was worth thinking about. Cameron held the roan on a tight rein, keeping the carbine aimed at Arker.

"If you were here, then you know what day Tod Purcell rode through your yard. Was it Monday or Tuesday?"

He threw the question out sharply, hoping to catch Arker off guard. But he saw he had failed. Arker said easily, "I got no time to keep track of a kid's comings and goings. Lots of riders went through here Saturday and Sunday — the quick trail to the high country goes up past my corral."

He took a step backwards, paused and gulped some beer. "Now get off my land, Cameron. This is private property, so ride out!"

"So was my steer private property," Cameron answered. "And the week I gave you is up. Pay me my fifty dollars and I'll ride."

Once more he saw that he had failed to jar Arker. And again the big man surprised him. He sounded almost amiable as he said, "You'll get your money when Obed pays me off for working the roundup. That'll be Monday morning."

Cameron stared speculatively across the small yard. What the devil was Arker up to, acting this way? While Cameron watched, Arker holstered his gun, finished his beer, and turned toward the door. He stepped inside and in a moment was back, his glass gone but his hat on his head. He walked toward his saddle horse and climbed aboard. It was his big palomino and he sat it proudly.

Leaning forward, he untied the reins of the pack horse and hooked them to his saddle. Then he freed the palomino and swung it away from the hitching rail.

Cameron remained where he was, the rifle moving as Arker moved. Arker reined up and scowled. "I ain't got time to fool with you now, Cameron. There's men waiting in the hills for this grub. But if you still got ideas that I jumped you Saturday, just remember this — when I get around to rousting you, it won't be in no dark alley. And you won't be getting out of bed in no few days neither. And I'll do the job myself — alone."

He started the horses up. "All I want is a

chance to get at you when you ain't got a gun poking at me. That's all — just one chance." His voice was thick and heavy with hatred. Not looking at Cameron further, he rode past him and up the trail into the hills.

Cameron sat where he was, watching Arker until he disappeared. The man's anger he had expected; it was his earlier attitude that Cameron found puzzling. And the words had come out hard — as if Arker hadn't wanted to say them but had been forced to.

As for the threat, Cameron was too experienced in the ways of men like Rafe Arker to take it lightly. He studied the hill trail, frowning. Tod had ridden that way. And from what little sign there was by the corral, Cameron guessed he was still being pressed hard when he climbed over the first hump and dropped out of sight.

Tod might still be in those hills, Cameron thought. He knew them as well as Jenny did, and given half a chance he could lead most men a will-o'-the-wisp chase as long as the strength of his horse held up well.

Cameron's first impulse was to move on into the hills. But there was another matter to check on first, and he swung the roan back toward the cut. He grinned a little sourly as he rode. Rafe Arker might take this to mean that he was keeping away from a fight. And Arker would be partly right. Cameron knew his own limitations. If he and the big man tangled now, Arker would grind him into the dirt. As if to disprove the thought, he tried lifting his right arm in a sharp upward movement. The pain shafted up from the torn muscles across his ribs, hitting him hard enough so that he nearly went sideways out of the saddle.

Cameron swore. He didn't like the idea of dodging a fight, but it looked as if he just might be doing that for some time yet. And because such thinking put a sour taste in his mouth, he forced his attention back to the job at hand.

He trailed the little paint easily up to the box canyon where the Dondees had their mine. He saw where Tod had left the horse and gone forward on foot. And he saw now that one set of hoofmarks was fresher than the others. The sign stood out sharp and clear in dirt kept moist by the shade from the rock shoulder. One horse had gone in not too long before, Cameron judged.

He moved his carbine so that the barrel lay across his saddle bow. But when he broke into the canyon there was no sign of life. A glittering pile of pyrites lay in the middle of the sun-baked yard, confirming Tod's guess. Now a jay appeared and chattered angrily at Cameron from the branches of a nearby pine. Insects began to click in the grass; and in the near distance something moved cautiously in the bushes near the mouth of the pine shaft.

Cameron frowned. Whoever had ridden in here hadn't gone back out. Yet there was no sign of him. The ground here was too baked to take prints. He looked around. Whoever it was could be in the cabin, or behind it; he could be in the mine shaft, carefully drawing his bead; or he could be up on the narrow, rocky trail that ran from the yard over a low hump and to the end of the canyon, where there was a woodlot.

He would be less of a target moving, Cameron thought sourly. He started the roan for the trail leading to the mine shaft. No one appeared above. There was no sound from up there. Cameron reined the roan to his left and put it onto the rocky trail leading to the woodlot.

The pitch was steep, and then it leveled off to make a wide hairpin loop and drop down over a low ridge. Cameron was squeezed by rock walls in the middle of the loop when Sax Larabee's softly mocking voice slashed razor sharp at him from above.

"You've got that gun aimed in the wrong direction, Roy. Keep it that way."

X

Cameron glanced up to see Larabee coming down toward him. He sat a rangy bay easily. He carried his .44 in his hand and when he reined in and leaned forward, he rested the barrel on the splayed top of the horn.

"From what that doctor of yours said, you aren't supposed to be up and around for two more days," Larabee said.

Cameron remained silent, waiting for Larabee to explain himself, his reason for being here.

His lack of response seemed to irritate Larabee. "What the devil are you doing riding on private land anyway?"

"Your land?"

Larabee's smile was amused. "In a manner of speaking. I'm the Dondees' silent partner."

Cameron nodded. "I judged as much. You set them on me Saturday night. Why?"

Larabee ignored the question. "You figured that out," he said. He laughed. "And you came hotfooting here looking for the Dondees?"

"I'll take care of them in good time,"

Cameron retorted. "I'm hunting Tod Purcell."

He saw the sudden and quickly hidden gleam touch Larabee's dark eyes, and he knew that his earlier guesses had been right. Larabee and the Dondee brothers had been the ones to chase Tod into the hills. Anger surged up despite Cameron's efforts to match Larabee's calmness. He said thickly, "If you've hurt that kid, Sax, I'll nail you to the wall."

Larabee stared at Cameron. He was obviously trying to make up his mind as to his next step, but when he spoke he sounded as sure of himself as if he'd never been faced with a decision.

"The kid's all right — or he was when I last heard. He's in the high country, holed up in a narrow-necked draw."

"And the Dondees are up there too — waiting for hunger to bring him to them?" Cameron's voice was still heavy, but he had some of his control back now.

"That's not your concern," Larabee said. He leaned forward. "Your job is to get back to that hospital bed. And stay in it until Saturday night."

Cameron stared at him almost stupidly. "You're giving me orders?"

Larabee's voice was cold fire, "I warned

you before. Now I'm making it plain. Do as I tell you or ride out of this country — now. Because if you buck, Roy, I'm telling Balder and Stedman and the rest of your town fathers that they have a jail-bird for a deputy marshal. That the man they plan on making kingpin spent time in the penitentiary."

"And they'll believe you?"

"I have proof," Larabee said. "They'll believe me."

And they would react just the way Larabee wanted them to. Balder and Stedman would even if the others were more charitable. But they were the two who counted the most. They were the ones whose disapproval would drive him from this country, from the land he owned, from the future he looked forward to — maybe even from Jenny Purcell.

Cameron continued to stare at Larabee. But now he was beginning to understand the breadth of the man's plan. He hadn't come here merely to revenge himself for what had happened those years back in Colorado. He had prepared for his coming too well.

Cameron said slowly, "You sent the Dondees here to see just how tough this country was."

Larabee acknowledged the accusation with a slight nod. "I found out about it before that — about you being here, about the big horse sale to the army, about the kind of men who run this country." He laughed. "Like Balder and Stedman and that fool Obed Beggs. Self-righteous fools, and greedy ones. They're the best kind, Roy. They can be handled easiest of all."

Cameron was only half listening. He was following his own train of thought. Larabee had come for the gold the army would leave behind. At the same time he wanted his revenge, wanted to wipe out the bitter taste he had nursed in himself all these years. And somehow, Cameron knew, he planned to make the two desires work together, to make the one help him get the other.

But how did he expect to get that money? The army men had a strong guard on it now. And when they were gone, it would be in the bank vaults, watched carefully by cautious townsmen during the day, by the law at night.

The realization of Larabee's intent jarred him like a blow to the belly. That was it! He was the law. And if he was up and around, he would be the Saturday night guard at the bank! His being there was the key to Larabee's whole plan.

And now he understood a good deal that had escaped him before. He said, "That's why you had me beaten up — to keep me out of action while you made your final plans. But your crew got a little too eager and you had to step in and stop them."

Larabee's expression revealed nothing. Cameron went on, "You put Rafe Arker up to fighting me that first night, and when he failed you brought in the Dondees."

He leaned forward now, his eyes slashing at Larabee's expressionless countenance. "You had it all worked out — how I'd either do what you wanted Saturday night and let you and your friends take the gold or you'd tell your story. You figured that would get me out of the way and make the robbery easier for you."

"Having you stand aside and wait would be the easiest," Larabee said calmly. "And that's what you'll do."

"And then what?" Cameron cried. "Then I stand convicted as a traitor to these people or as a fool, not worth a lawman's hire!"

"No," Larabee said. "You've been beat. You'll look like you put up a fight but that you didn't have the strength to win. No one will hold anything against you." He smiled, a sardonic twist of his mouth. "You'll be marshal someday, Roy. You can marry that girl, raise your stock, grow old and fat here. That's what I'm offering you — security."

It was possible, Cameron thought. Larabee was clever enough to do this. But security in exchange for what? A bleak winter for the ranchers and the townsmen — and failure for some of them living now on hope of the army's gold. That and the life of a boy who had once been on the edge of wildness and who had stepped back, drawn by his admiration for Cameron.

Security in exchange for scars he would carry inside himself the rest of his life.

Larabee's voice slashed like a bullwhip. "You've had your talk, Roy. Now ride back to town like I told you."

Cameron ignored the order. "I came looking for Tod Purcell," he said. "I'll go nowhere without him."

Larabee smiled thinly. "The little snoop overheard me talking to the Dondees. He knows about you, Roy — all about you. If you're wise, you'll leave him to my men to take care of."

Cameron remained twisted in the saddle, staring at Larabee. His carbine was

aimed still at nothing, and the fact of
Larabee's gun loomed large in his con-
sciousness. He was tired and his body
ached from the strain these last few hours
had put on it. His mind slid easily to the
obvious solution — agree with Larabee.
Agree to go back to town and wait; agree
to stand aside on Saturday night. And then
when the trap was set, when Larabee and
his crew were deep inside, spring that trap.

Cameron had long ago learned to fight
the lawless with their own weapons whenever he needed to. But he turned away
from this plan quickly. Once he rode away
from here — once he crawled back to town
— he had signed and sealed Tod Purcell's
death warrant. Larabee had admitted
Tod's overhearing him. He couldn't afford
to risk the boy's getting loose. His whole
scheme depended on surprise — and on
Cameron. The one he could destroy and
still have a chance. The other he dared not
risk losing.

"When I ride back to town, Tod rides
with me," Cameron said softly.

Color flooded Larabee's cheeks as he
fought impatience, surging anger. "I've
given you all the time you needed. I can
kill you now and still get the money." His
eyes glittered. "Don't try to bluff me, Roy.

I've thought this all out. If you force me to kill you, nothing changes. Nothing except that you won't be found. And after the money's found missing, who do you think the law will hunt for? You — once they hear you spent time in prison for bank robbery."

There was no lightness, no mockery left in him. He sat the bay horse with his frame shaking from suppressed rage at this man daring to flout him. His arm quivered and the gun muzzle chattered softly on the leather covering of the saddle horn.

And he was back where he had started, Cameron realized. He had the same choice offered him when Larabee first got the drop on him, long moments ago. He could try to beat that .44 aimed at his body or he could turn and ride.

"You leave me nothing, Sax," he said in a complaining voice. With a grimace, he lifted the carbine, raising the butt high and swinging the barrel around and down the open mouth of the boot.

He could feel Larabee's tautness. He had no need to look to know that Larabee's finger was tight on the trigger of the gun, that his body was ready for instant response if Cameron should make his try now. Cameron hadn't lied — Larabee had left him nothing.

The tip of the carbine was almost brushing the leather of the boot opening. Cameron sucked in a short, harsh breath, knowing that the necessary suddenness of his next move would send pain slashing through his body. It would roar up from his torn ribs to explode in his gun arm.

As he let out the breath, he drove his elbow close to his side and levered the carbine barrel up with his forearm. His head came up and he saw the glint of understanding form in Larabee's eyes. He tried to fling himself to one side and fire the carbine at the same time. He heard the crash of Larabee's .44 blend with the crack of his carbine. Blackness blinded him, and he thought, "I've lost!"

XI

Cameron felt the strong pull of the stirrup against his left ankle. Vaguely he realized that he was hanging far over on the right side of the roan and that it was dancing crazily, trying to back out of the narrow confines of this trail. With an effort that sent a new surge of pain slashing through him, Cameron forced himself back into the saddle.

His vision cleared. He heard the shrill neigh of a frightened horse and he saw Larabee's bay plunging with the same wildness that gripped the roan. Larabee was fighting with one hand to control the horse; the other still held his gun and he strained to bring it to bear on Cameron again. A bright red streak on the bay's flank told clearly where the carbine bullet had gone.

But Larabee was a superb horseman, Cameron knew. In a moment he would have the animal under control and be able to bring his gun into play. Cameron could feel the numbness that blotted all feeling from his right side. The emptiness ran the length of his arm, leaving him barely enough strength to hold the carbine. Moving as quickly as he could manage, he took the gun with his left hand and thrust it into the boot. For an instant, the roan was free of restraint and he sunfished, nearly pitching Cameron over his head.

Then Cameron had a grip on the reins and he brought the frightened horse under control with a harsh movement of his wrist. Momentarily he was motionless in the saddle. He could feel heat like a branding iron across his back and guessed that Larabee's bullet had scoured his vest, blistering the flesh underneath. He saw that Larabee nearly had the bay steady again and he made an effort to draw his hand gun. But his right arm hung uselessly, refusing to move, and he knew that again he had no choice.

He reined the roan about violently. Its hindquarters scraped rock and then it was heading downtrail, snorting its displeasure. Cameron sent it cantering downslope, into the box canyon, and across the sun-hot dirt where the glittering heap of pyrites still lay. He heard Larabee's cry behind him and a bullet slashed through the air to whip at his hatbrim. Then he was plunging out of the canyon onto the short trail that led to the wagonroad.

This was the way Tod must have bolted, he thought — but with three after him instead of just one. And Tod had managed to get away. Somehow he had eluded all three riders and made his way into the high country. From Larabee's words, Cameron guessed that Tod was holed up where he could defend himself but where he couldn't leave.

Cameron's knowledge of the high country was limited. He knew only the few places Jenny had shown him on their infrequent rides. She had taken him to tucked away meadows — secret places, she called them, where she and her brother and Tod had hunted before her brother's death. It was a place such as one of these that she planned to go after the wild horses, Cameron thought; and it would be the same kind of place Tod would have headed for.

He looked back to see Larabee barely within handgun range. He tried again to command his right arm to move but it hung lifelessly, flopping with the motion of the roan. Cameron drove his heels into the horse, lifting its gait to a dangerous pace here on the steep downslope. To his right, the timber looked inviting. But he thrust the temptation from his mind. He would gain nothing by holding up there. His one chance to help Tod would be to ride for the high country and try to break him free of the trap he had probably ridden himself into.

The rutted track leading to Rafe Arker's place loomed on the left. As Cameron swung toward it, a bullet whined in his direction, much of its force spent by distance. He slowed the roan briefly, allowing it to gain footing on this different terrain, and then he urged it to speed again. Sand spurted from under the flying hoofs as they raced through the stand of scrub pine. Shoes rang on rock as they sliced through the twisting cut. Then Cameron burst into Arker's yard. It was empty, and the feel of desolation reminded him that Arker had gone ahead into the hills.

Ahead lay the rock-hard ground of the first hills. Behind, the beat of hoofs warned that the bay was close. Cameron sent the roan up a steep slope, down into a narrow gully, and along the hard-packed trail toward the mountains rising close ahead.

Lead slashed the air behind him as Larabee fired. But for the moment he had the distance, and the shot fell short. He kept the roan driving, hating this as he heard the horse's breath begin to gust, as he felt the foam of sweat lathering its sides.

Now the first timber appeared and a coolness touched the air. The trail broke onto a flat and the roan shied. Cameron swore. Halfway across the flat Rafe Arker rode his palomino, the pack horse ambling along behind. The roan drew even and then was past. Arker lifted his head, gasping as Cameron charged by. From behind, came Larabee's shrill cry, "Get him, you fool! Gun him down!"

Arker's answer was a shout of pure pleasure. Cameron twisted around to see the big body settling in the saddle, to see sunlight glinting on a swiftly drawn gun barrel. He turned back. He had to find refuge soon. In an open race, the long-legged palomino could run the little roan into the ground. Three or four trails wound across the flat and into canyon openings at the far end. One half blocked by a rock slide caught Cameron's eye. Faintly he recalled Jenny leading him around that slide. He reined the roan slightly to the left, swung it around the tumble of rocks, and disappeared into the shadow cast by the canyon walls. Arker's gun slammed viciously behind him, sending lead shrilling off rock. Then the twists in the canyon carried him to momentary safety.

He rode a good two hundred yards, hearing nothing but the heavy breathing of the roan and the beat of its hoofs on the hard floor of the canyon. Then the echo of other horses coming reached his ears. Cameron sought to remember what lay ahead, to recall any possible way to throw his pursuers off the track. He swore as he realized that Rafe Arker would know this country all too well. If Larabee had been alone, he might be fooled. But there was no chance of that with Arker to guide him.

And now Cameron felt the roan stumble. He slowed its pace and looked ahead. The canyon was widening. Beyond it, he could see a kink of trail winding steeply up the mountainside, and he knew that he would have to rest the roan soon. Its heart would burst under the effort of running up those pitches ahead.

Now Cameron caught a glimpse of red rock on his left, of a tiny spring trickling down the hillside on his right, of a strange formation half blocking the sly ahead — and memory surged back. A short distance on, the canyon branched into three trails. One was a cul-de-sac, but the other two eventually met higher up. The right-hand fork was the longer, he recalled. It wound its way through a thick stand of trees and across the sharpness of flint rock. And because it was the poorer of the two trails, he just might throw Rafe Arker off by taking it — if he could get past the first bend without being seen. Then he could chance resting the roan in a small clearing by a spring where he and Jenny had once stopped to cook coffee.

The beginning of the trail loomed close. Cameron looked back. The twisting canyon showed empty for the moment. Quickly, he spurred the roan up the right fork. It stumbled over flinty ground, dropped down a short slope and then moved around the first bend. And now Cameron took the pressure off, letting the horse find its own gait.

The trees began a short distance ahead. It would be somewhere within the next quarter mile that he would find the clearing, he recalled. He watched the trees close in, casting their shadows, bringing the coolness that lay ahead with the night. They were big trees, with thick boles and great tangles of branches. A thick carpet of their needles lay over the trail, undisturbed for some time. Now he caught a glimpse of a long-cut butt and he remembered that it had been Jenny's signpost. A moment after, he saw the thin break in the buckbrush clumped under the trees and he edged the roan through and on a short distance to the small grassy clearing he sought.

Leaving the saddle, Cameron tied the roan away from the small pool at the edge of the clearing and walked back to the break in the brush. He was thinking of covering his tracks here where he had turned off the trail but he saw that this would not help him at all. The roan's hoofs had scuffed the pine needles all along the trail to this point. Wearily, Cameron hurried back to the roan and mounted it again. Returning to the trail, he rode up it a good fifty yards. Here the trees ended and the ground was flinty again, too hard to show any sign.

Now Cameron slid from the saddle and led the horse. He angled into the trees, careful not to put any more sign on the pine needles. It was slow, tiring work, finding room enough through the thick stand of timber and through the brush to lead the roan. But finally he was back in the clearing. Tying the animal again, he returned to the place where he had first left the trail and smoothed away any sign of his turning off here. It was far from a perfect job, he knew, but it might be enough to keep Rafe Arker away those few extra minutes the roan needed to recover its strength.

The horse had cooled down when Cameron returned to the clearing, and now he let it drink. He set it to grazing on the grass and stretched out, his face to the sky, and tried to nurse some feeling back into his numbed right side.

The silence here was broken only by the soft sounds of the roan eating and by the occasional cry of a bird. Arker and Larabee had taken the other trail. But Cameron knew they wouldn't be fooled for long. Once Arker realized there was no sign on the trail he was following, he would know what had happened.

Cameron kneaded his right arm with his left hand. Feeling came back — dull pain at first, and then sharp shoots that brought the sweat out on his body. Slowly he lifted his right shoulder, feeling the cramped, bruised muscles across his ribs draw out reluctantly. He began to move his arm higher, quicker, teeth clenched against the pain lancing through him. But he felt the looseness coming, the hard, sharp spasms lessening, and he knew that until he had another shock like the one by the Dondee mine, he was fit again.

Now he heard the jangle of harness. He glanced at the roan. It was still drooping a little but some of the strength had come back to its muscles if the speed of its eating had any meaning. Turning away, Cameron eased through the brush until he was almost at the edge of the trail. He could hear them coming, their voices carrying over the soft plopping sounds of hoofs against the pine needles.

"He didn't take the other trail so he must have taken this one," Rafe Arker was rumbling.

"I still think us both coming here was a fool thing to do," Sax Larabee answered. "One of us should have stayed on the other trail. If it's as much shorter as you claim, we could have blocked him where the two meet."

"No," Arker said. "I know these trails; you don't. There are too many places along here for Cameron to hide and pick one of us off. If we're together, he'll think twice before chancing a fight." He gave his rough laugh. "As for him getting ahead far, I ain't worried. That roan was about beat when it hit the flat. It'll play out sooner or later. Then we'll have him."

They moved on past at a steady pace, and soon a bend took them out of sight.

Cameron sat quietly, trying to recall just how much more of this trail there was up to where it met the other, shorter one. A good mile beyond the end of the trees, he thought. Not so far as distance went, but achingly slow because of the terrain. He could go back and take the other trail and with any luck be past the fork ahead before Arker and Larabee reached it.

Hurrying back to the roan, he mounted and rode to the trail. He turned downslope, and the roan moved easily now that it had no upgrade to pull.

Cameron slapped it lightly on the neck. His arm was functioning again. The roan was somewhat rested. He felt for the first time that he might have a chance to reach the high country ahead of Arker and Larabee.

He came to the foot of the trail, rode along the bottom of a bluff and turned up the other trail. It was the one he had seen from the canyon. For the first quarter mile it kinked openly up the hillside. But then it leveled off and it ran only slightly sloping the rest of the distance to the fork.

He was over the grade and trotting the roan along a packed dirt trail when another memory came back to him. A short distance beyond the fork, the trail crossed a swampy spot. Arker would see that Cameron had left no sign there and he would realize he had been tricked.

And then he and Larabee would come back. And this time, Cameron guessed, each man would take a branch of the trail, searching for him with gun drawn. His only chance was to reach the soft ground first.

He looked ahead. This trail ran over small, open flats. It ran through smooth-sided cuts. But nowhere did it cut into a stand of timber. Nowhere was there a place for a man to hide. His one chance then was to push the roan again. To reach the fork and get beyond it, beyond the swampy spot, before Arker and Larabee could realize they had him trapped.

And once more he dug his heels into the tiring horse's flanks.

XII

They began to angle sharply eastward and Cameron knew that the junction of the two trails lay not far ahead. He rounded a shoulder of rock and there was the fork. He swung in the saddle, looking back. From here he could see some distance down the other trail. There was no sign of life yet. He glanced ahead. The trail lay exposed as it worked up to the lip of a high bench. It was empty.

Cameron squinted westward at the sun. It was sliding for the distant hills. It wouldn't be too long now before dusk came to this high country, and with it would be the mountain chill. Now, while he still had light and while Larabee and Arker were still behind him, was the time to make as much speed as he could to put precious distance between himself and his pursuers. But the roan was staggering again. He wouldn't be able to carry Cameron's weight much longer.

"Make it to the bench, fellow," he murmured.

The roan kept moving, but its pace was

slow now, almost a walk. Halfway up the slope toward the bench, Cameron looked back. He saw the two riders reach the fork. They paused. Then a hand lifted and pointed toward him.

The swampy ground lay just ahead and Cameron turned his attention to getting the roan through it. When he was on the far side, he looked back again. Larabee and Arker had cut down the distance more than he had expected. He would be lucky to get halfway across the bench before they caught up with him.

He had hoped to reach the timber beyond the bench, using the thick stand of spruce and high country fir as a refuge. But he made no effort now to hurry the roan. It would respond, he knew, and at this altitude going too fast would burst its heart.

The lip of the bench lay just ahead. Once Cameron glanced over his shoulder. Arker and his big palomino were in the lead, almost within handgun range. The roan strained itself and came up onto the level ground. Cameron reined it in and dropped to the trail.

"You rest a minute," he said softly.

Pulling the carbine from the saddle boot, he stepped to the beginning of the downslope. He lifted the gun carefully, testing his own reactions. He could feel the pull of his rib muscles, but his arm functioned well enough. Now he sighted carefully, drawing his bead on Arker's bobbing hat. He caught the rhythm of the palomino's gait and when Arker went up in the saddle, he fired.

His bullet took a tuft of felt from the crown of the hat. Arker flattened in the saddle. Cameron fired again, this time driving his shot in front of the palomino, forcing it to rear up. He saw Arker claw for leather with the horse's unexpected movement. Then he had control again, but the big animal was standing still now.

Cameron moved back out of sight. He eased along the rim of the bench until he found a screen of bushes. He bellied down there and slipped his gun barrel through the tangle of leaves. He could see Arker, with Larabee alongside him now. They were coming hard up the trail.

Cameron fired three quick shots, driving lead into the ground in front of the horses, forcing their riders to fight for control. Arker and Larabee stopped. Then they came on, guns drawn. Cameron ticked the air close to Larabee, and again the two men stopped.

He saw them squint toward the sun and he chuckled softly. This was what he wanted — to force them to wait until darkness to come after him. He fired again and then sat up to reload.

From below someone shot. Cameron heard the bullets strike the slope well below him, and he kept on with his reloading. Then he bellied down again and studied the situation. Larabee and Arker were riding apart, making two targets instead of one. And they were coming on once more.

Cameron began shooting. He could not bring himself to kill in a situation like this. It would be murder, little different from shooting them in the back. The law had been grained into him too long. With the odds even, he would shoot to kill — if they attacked first. Until then, he worked to gain the time he needed.

The pattern of lead he laid down brought both riders to a halt again. Now he sent his shots closer. They turned and rode out of easy range. And here they left their saddles. Cameron laughed out loud. It looked as if he had got the time he needed.

He crawled backward until he could stand up with no risk of being seen. Hurrying to the roan, he took the reins and led it forward. He lifted his head to find the timber and judge how long it would take him to reach that temporary safety.

There were no trees at the end of the

bench. They showed in the distance, at the back of a second bench that lay behind this one like a giant step. Cameron swore. His memory had tricked him, blending the two flats into one. And the width of this bench shook him. Leading the roan at this pace, it would be dark before he reached the far side.

He walked until he decided the roan had had rest enough. Mounting, he rode at a fair pace until he could feel the animal tiring again. Then he left the saddle and began walking once more. The last of the sun disappeared as he reached the foot of the short, steep trail that led up to the higher bench. Cameron paused to look back. The trail was empty. But it wouldn't be for long. Men like Larabee and Rafe Arker couldn't be bluffed forever. As soon as they risked moving into gun range by the lip of the bench, they would know he was no longer up there with his carbine. Then they would come on fast enough.

Cameron walked the roan to the top of the trail. On level ground once more, he climbed into the saddle. His days in bed had begun to tell on him. The strain of that last steep quarter mile had drained him. He looked ahead in the dusky light, blinking to clear his swimming vision.

The timber looked frighteningly far

away. But halfway across the bench and a good twenty yards to the right of the trail was a tumble of boulders. He angled toward them and saw that they hung on the edge of a drop-off that fell into a canyon shrouded in darkness.

The roan stumbled. Cameron said wearily, "It's the end of the ride for both of us," and slid out of the saddle.

He studied the tumble of rocks. Some of them were huge, great chunks of granite tossed and left here by some ancient glacier. He found two leaning together, forming a half cave. Behind them, shielded from the trail, was a tiny clearing, grassy thanks to a seep of water. Leading the roan into the clearing, Cameron stripped off its gear and put it on a short picket line. Then he took the carbine and climbed laboriously to the top of a nearby flat rock. He lay quietly, looking through the dusk downtrail.

Darkness came and with it the icy fingers of cold air probing down from the mountain peaks looming up behind the timber. Cameron felt his side stiffening. He would need fire, he realized. Tired as he was, he had little enough resistance. At this height, pneumonia could catch him before the night was out.

He used the last of the dusk to spot a

deadfall hanging on the rim of the canyon at his back. It was some distance away and getting to it meant stumbling over rocky ground. Then he had to drop over the edge of the canyon and break off those branches thin enough to give in to his draining strength. By the time he started back, it was full dark, with only the bright, hard stars for light, and he nearly missed the refuge of rocks. The whinny of the roan, asking for company and comfort, turned him at the right moment, and finally he was under the stony canopy, talking to the horse and half collapsed on top of his pile of wood.

After a time he managed to stir and build a small fire. He had no food except the small emergency ration he had long ago learned to keep in his saddlebags — bread, cheese and a handful of coffee along with the can to cook it in. The bread was stale after its days of lying in the leather bag, and the cheese was sweaty from the hot sun. But he managed a meal, washing it down with coffee gulped out of the can.

He kept the fire small, both to save wood and to keep it from being seen if Arker and Larabee should reach the bench tonight. But the rock walls on two sides caught the heat and threw it back and so he felt it driving the mountain chill out of reach.

When the moon rose, he climbed to the flat-topped rock and looked down the trail. Nothing moved along it. A faint glow in the distance and well below his level caught his eye. A fire down on the other bench! Cameron crawled back to his half cave and readied himself for sleep.

The clink of metal on rock and the feel of the ground trembling under the stride of something heavy brought him dazedly to his feet. He gaped at the gray light seeping in around him. He realized that it was well past dawn. His tired body had betrayed him. He had slept a good hour past the point of safety.

Quickly now he squirmed up the flat-topped rock. Arker and Larabee had come, as he feared. They were approaching the tumble of rocks — but not from below. They came from the direction of the timber. It took him a moment to realize what had happened. Then he understood. They had ridden on past the rocks, thinking he had got as far as the timber. But Arker must have noticed the lack of sign at the edge of the trees, where the dirt would be soft from heavy shade. It would not have taken Larabee long to spot the rocks and guess that Cameron was hiding in them.

They led the pack pony now and Cameron guessed that Arker had left it somewhere along the trail earlier and gone back for it before making camp last night. The big pack bulged and Cameron thought hungrily of the food that must be in it.

Then the nearness of the two men brought his mind back to the reality of the moment. He swore as he realized he had left the carbine below. Awkwardly he drew his handgun and rested the barrel on a small upthrust of rock in front of him. They stopped suddenly, still out of range of his forty-four, and he wondered if they had seen him.

Then he saw Larabee glance behind himself, eastward. The first hint of the rising sun shone behind the peaks in that direction. Larabee leaned toward Arker and spoke at length. Arker's big body shook and Cameron heard his laughter boom out, carried clearly on the still, cold air.

Cameron frowned, wondering what their plan might be. He guessed that they were sure he was in the rocks, and that they were staying well away until the right moment came to move in.

The sun topped a ridge, and now Cameron saw Larabee's strategy. The brightness struck Cameron full in the face, blinding him from seeing anything straight ahead. He had a blurred glimpse of Arker making a wide swing to the left and Larabee following suit to the right. He fired, knowing it was a hopeless act as he pulled the trigger.

Even if he could have seen through the bright light of the sun, he could not handle both men at the same time. One of them was bound to make it close enough to the rocks to be out of range — unless he was willing to risk stepping into the open for a showdown. And, he knew, with the sun behind them, Larabee and Arker held the long end of the odds.

The chatter of hoofs on rock and the shaking of the ground as the bay and the big palomino plunged toward the rocks told Cameron what was happening. He ducked his head to the side, away from the blinding sunlight. He looked to his left, one hand up to shield his eyes. He had a glimpse of Arker and the palomino, with the pack horse stumbling along behind, duck into shadow and disappear. They would be close to the rocks now, too close for Cameron to see them from his position. He twisted to his right. Larabee was coming up fast on the bay. Cameron fired at him. Larabee answered, spraying the rock with lead, forcing Cameron to lie flat. Then Larabee was also too close in to be an effective target.

Cameron dropped off the rock and into the half cave. There was only one way in here, along a topless tunnel stretching eastward. As long as his bullets held out, they couldn't reach him.

Nor could he reach them, he realized.

He grinned sourly. It was stalemate.

And then he remembered — there were two of them to take turns standing guard. He was only one, and sooner or later he would have to sleep. And they had the food. He had only an empty belly.

From beyond the end of the tunnel, Larabee's voice came clear and mocking: "You might as well come out now, Roy. You've got nothing to wait for. Not anymore."

Cameron squatted down with his back to the rock wall. From this position he could see the yellow splotch of sunlight at the mouth of the tunnel. Anyone coming after him would have to step through the sunlight and into shadow. He would have a perfectly outlined target while his opponent would be temporarily blinded by the dimness.

It was his round — as long as he could stay right here.

XIII

Larabee and Arker stayed out of sight of the tunnel mouth. They moved around restlessly, talking in low tones. Cameron could hear everything they said and did — the tunnel sucked in sound and carried it to him plainly. He listened to them set up camp — building a fire and starting coffee cooking. His stomach growled at the rich odor.

From the sharpness in Larabee's voice, Cameron realized that his patience was wearing thin. Cameron wondered if he could keep Larabee that way. If so, he might have a chance. An impatient man was a man who made mistakes.

Larabee said, "I can't spend any more time here. I have to get to town."

"You got all day and half the night before we hit the bank," Rafe Arker said. "We'll get both Cameron and the kid in plenty of time."

"Remember, Cameron was going to stand guard," Larabee said. "When he played the fool and refused, I thought we'd have to take all the risk ourselves. But now I've figured something that might even be better than the original plan."

"It better be good," Arker warned. "I ain't going to risk passing up my share of that gold. I got plans for it. After this winter is over, the man who's got money'll be able to buy up half the valley. And that's going to be me. Without the gold, there ain't many ranchers who can ride through another year."

"It is good," Larabee assured him. "And it solves all our problems — Cameron, the kid, those fools in town getting suspicious of us." He laughed abruptly. "By the time Cameron and the kid are found — if they ever are — it'll be too late for anybody to do anything. Meanwhile, those Cougar Hill yokels can spend their time hunting for Cameron to arrest him for robbing the bank!"

Arker's grunt was skeptical. "By God," he said, "I'd like to see you make Balder and the rest think Cameron ain't a little tin god."

"That's why I have to get to town before long," Larabee said. A lazy chuckle replaced some of the sharpness in his voice. "How did you think I was going to get Cameron to stand guard for us tonight?"

Arker made no reply. Larabee went on,

"Because I told him I'd spread the word about his having been in prison. You know how Balder would take that!"

"He'd throw you out of his office," Rafe Arker said.

"Hardly. Because I have proof," Larabee purred. "I have a copy of the record that was made when they arrested Cameron." His chuckle grew stronger. "By the time I finish with my story, every man in town will be on the lookout for him. Even if he managed to get away from us, he wouldn't find much help in these parts — not after I get through with him."

"He ain't going to get away," Arker rumbled. He grunted again. "But I don't see what good all this is going to do. If you got everybody on the lookout for Cameron, you won't be able to get within a mile of that bank tonight. It'll be surrounded by guards three deep."

"That's right, it would be," Larabee agreed complacently. "But not tonight. Because I'm going to tell Stedman and Balder that I overheard Cameron and a pair of strangers planning to hit the bank tomorrow night — when everybody was off-guard. I'll explain that until I heard the talk, I didn't think it my business to expose Cameron's past. But now I have no choice, since I'm a very law-abiding man."

He went on, obviously pleased with himself, "Don't forget, Arker, that in the eyes of men like Stedman and his friends, I'm a first class citizen. A wealthy businessman. And to Stedman's type, that kind can do no wrong.

"Besides, some of the money in that bank is mine — a good faith deposit I made when I first came here. It's only logical that I try to protect it."

"Even so," Arker argued, "that don't mean Balder'll have any fewer guards around the bank tonight than he will tomorrow."

"Don't be a fool," Larabee said with impatience. "This is Saturday. Tonight, all the crews that have come down out of the hills will be celebrating. The army will have taken away all but the last few head of stock and the bank will be full of gold everybody plans to get on Monday. By midnight, how many men will be sober enough to stand guard for Balder?"

"A pair in front, maybe. Two in the alley for sure," Arker said.

"Exactly. And those two in the alley are going to be relieved just before one o'clock in the morning. By the Dondee brothers, or one of them and Farley."

"If they don't want to be relieved, what then?"

"We'll take care of them," Larabee said. "Remember, they'll see only two men. But I'll be there too. And three against a pair is pretty fair odds."

"What about me?" Arker asked. His voice thickened slightly with suspicion.

"I told you before I didn't want you in town," Larabee snapped. "Anybody would recognize you and that palomino two blocks off. You and one of the Dondees or Farley will have camp set up in that hideout over the south pass that you told me about."

"You better have Joe with you," Arker said. "He and me are the only ones can find that place."

"As soon as we get the gold," Larabee said, "we'll ride up and hide it — where each of us can watch the others. Then you and Farley hit for your ranch and the Dondees for their mine. I'll circle in the hills and come out by Obed Beggs' place, claiming I was hunting for Cameron. When things quiet down, we'll help ourselves to the gold and each can go his own way."

Larabee's shadow fell across the mouth of the tunnel. "Now you see why Cameron and the kid have to be got rid of — and hidden so they won't turn up before spring at the earliest."

162

"I'll take care of them," Arker said. "As soon as Joe shows up, you ride for town and leave Cameron and the kid to him and me."

"Farley's supposed to be watching that Purcell girl," Larabee said. "And she should be on her way into the mountains by now. I understand she was going to the meadow above to bring down the last of the wild stuff."

"You told Joe to watch Jenny?" Arker sounded angry. "What for?"

"Because where she plans to go is the place where the Dondees have the kid holed up — at least it's a meadow with wild horses in it. And she knows these mountains. What if she gets wind that the boy is there? She might trick the Dondees and get the kid away. I'm taking no chances at this stage."

"Nobody fools with Jenny," Arker said. "When I'm owner of half a dozen ranches, I got a feeling she'll think different about me than she does now."

Cameron smiled thinly at the big man's simplicity. Then the smile faded as he heard Larabee say very softly, "And what if it comes to a choice between the girl and the gold?"

Arker was silent for some time. Then he

said, "A woman's easier to get than gold, Larabee. But there ain't no call to gun her down. I know these mountains too, remember. If she shows up, you leave me handle her." His voice thickened. "Maybe I can find out today how she'll like me when I'm rich."

Larabee swore with sudden, deep pleasure. "That's the way to do it!" he exclaimed. "When she shows up, we'll catch her and give you the job of guarding her. How do you think Cameron will act when he learns that?"

Arker's laugh rumbled through the tunnel. "By God! He'll come outa them rocks like a scalded goat!" he cried.

"And once we get Cameron out of the way, we'll use the same trick on the kid," Larabee went on quickly. "He's been hanging around Cameron long enough to be the same kind of damn fool."

He raised his voice. "Roy, can you hear me? Jenny's coming up this way. I'm going to catch her and give her to Arker for safe-keeping."

Anger shook Cameron. He knew that Larabee meant every word he said. This was the kind of solution he would think of, the kind of plan his cold, twisted mind would conceive. And what he said was true

— both Tod and Cameron would risk themselves to keep Jenny away from Rafe Arker.

"Well, Roy . . . ?"

"Someone's coming onto the bench," Arker warned.

There was a scrambling sound as someone climbed up the rocks to get a better view. Cameron heard Larabee's voice, fainter now. "It's the girl!"

Cameron heard the sound of his sliding down the rocks. "Pull the horses in behind that boulder," he ordered. "Keep out of her sight for a while. But stay by your palomino. Then as soon as she's abreast of us, you angle up toward the timber and block her. If she tries to turn, I'll be in the way."

His laughter seemed to choke him. "And then watch Cameron come out of here — like a cork out of a bottle of wild champagne!"

"When he does, I want him," Arker said savagely. "Remember that — Cameron's mine!"

"Of course," Larabee answered. He was still laughing. "You can have Cameron and the girl both!"

XIV

Cameron's impulse was to run down the tunnel and fight it out with Larabee and Arker. But he forced himself to calmness. He could still not handle himself easily — the threat of that surging, numbing pain was ever-present. His only hope of success would lie in surprise, and he knew they would hear him coming and be waiting.

As quickly as he could manage, he turned and made his way to the base of the flat-topped rock he had used before as a lookout. He climbed to the edge and then carefully lifted his head. Arker and Larabee were still too close to the rock pile for him to see, but Jenny was plainly visible.

She came along the bench trail at a steady pace, not driving her sorrel horse but not letting it linger either. Cameron's experienced glance took in the bulging saddlebags, the warbag tied behind the saddle, and he judged that she was too heavily laden to outrun the palomino unless she had a strong lead on it.

He scanned the trail ahead of Jenny. She

was almost halfway to the timber now and that part of the trail lying in front of her was level and fairly smooth. If she could make the timber, she could hold Arker off — she handled a carbine better than most men. But the angle Arker would ride from the rocks to the trail gave him all the advantage since Jenny would be lucky to see him before he was over halfway to her.

Cameron thought, If he could warn her now, she could turn and ride back. To catch her then, Larabee would have to run over rocky ground and with the sun in his eyes. Cameron gathered himself to rise up and shout his warning. The sound choked back in his throat. Coming over the crest of the bench behind Jenny was the unmistakable figure of Joe Farley. If she turned now, she would be caught between him and Larabee.

Her only hope was to outrun Rafe Arker. Cameron heaved to his feet. He stood openly, his hands cupped to his mouth. "Jenny, ride!" he cried. "Ride for the timber. Arker's in these rocks. Ride!"

He saw her head turn. He could almost see the surprise and bewilderment on her face. Then Arker's big palomino burst into view, racing at an angle toward the trail. At the same time, Arker was swiveled in the saddle so that he faced Cameron. Sunlight glinted harshly on the gun he held. He fired and lead screamed off the rock a foot to Cameron's right.

Cameron saw Larabee riding out on the left and knew that he was getting in position so they could pin him in a crossfire. His showing himself this way was what Larabee had anticipated. But Larabee had failed to count on one thing, Cameron saw — Jenny Purcell.

Instead of riding up the trail for the timber, she had turned her sorrel and was spurring it toward the rocks. Her carbine was out of its boot, and even as Cameron bellied down and tried to take aim on Arker's huge figure, she had the gun to her shoulder and was firing.

The palomino jerked to one side as dirt spurted by his hoofs. Cameron's shot missed as the horse jumped. Then he turned his attention to Larabee and sent two quick shots. He was no longer trying merely to drive Larabee away. Now he shot to kill. But even as he fired he could feel his arm fail to hold steady and his bullets went wide of their mark.

Joe Farley was coming in now, pushing his horse hard, unlimbering his gun as he came.

Cameron rose to his knees. Arker had the palomino straightened out and he was driving it toward Jenny's sorrel. "Ride for the timber!" Cameron cried at her.

Larabee's lead whined close to him. Another bullet ricocheted off rock, sending sharp shards against his side to rip at his clothes. He saw one of Jenny's shots send Larabee racing away in a wide arc. Cameron swore. With his shooting as poor as it was, he had little chance to help her at this range. And within minutes, the trio could close her in the middle of a deadly triangle. She might get one of them, but she had no chance against all three.

He could only help, Cameron realized, by getting out there, by being at close enough range to make his shooting count. He felt a bullet tug at his hatbrim as he slid backward off the rock. Then he was down in the small meadow, reaching for his saddle.

The roan was rested and fed and full of ginger. He tried a little bucking as Cameron mounted. "Save your energy," Cameron cautioned. He reloaded his .44 and spurred the roan for the tunnel.

His hope lay in surprise, but he dared not risk any more delay. He sent the horse spurting onto the rock-strewn plain. Jenny still held Arker and Larabee off with her carbine, but Joe Farley was coming within handgun range at her rear.

"Ride for the timber!" Cameron commanded her again. He drove a shot at Rafe Arker, forcing him to swing the palomino away from Jenny, giving her a chance to ride the angle Arker had planned to take. And now she went, leaning forward in the saddle, urging the sorrel to as much speed as it could muster with the load it carried.

Cameron saw Larabee come toward him. Arker turned at the same time. "Get the girl, Joe!" he cried.

Farley swung in Jenny's direction. Cameron saw her rein up. He groaned. Then he saw her strategy. She was out of handgun range now, but her carbine could reach to Larabee and Arker closing in on Cameron.

Her voice came across the flat: "Ride, Roy. It's your only chance!"

He could feel the roan's taut muscles under him. It wanted to run — then he'd let it run! He put his heels to its flanks and gave the horse its head. The stocky animal spurted forward. Both Larabee and Arker were coming in at an angle toward Cameron. The roan went between them and was a good dozen strides away before they could turn their mounts. Cameron let Jenny's carbine do the talking for him now. He concentrated on guiding the roan across the rocky ground. At the same time, he kept his eye on Farley.

Farley was almost within range of Jenny now and Cameron lifted his gun. The muscles of his right arm jumped, making sharp aim impossible. But his bullets were close enough to slow Farley long enough for Cameron to send the roan between him and Jenny.

And now Jenny turned the sorrel. Cameron dropped in behind her. Farley was coming on again. Arker and Larabee had their mounts driving, and the big palomino was beginning to eat up the ground in great gulps. Soon they would be within handgun range again, Cameron saw. Only the timber ahead offered any hope of safety.

Cameron laid a shot in front of the palomino. It broke stride, caught itself and pounded on again. To the left, Farley cried, "The girl's getting into the trees!"

Cameron looked up. The sorrel's tail flicked out of sight as the horse carried Jenny into the stand of spruce and alpine fir. Then a bullet scoured leather on his saddle and he twisted about. Arker and the palomino loomed large before his gaze. The bright sun picked out the steel of Arker's gun barrel and sent the bright reflection bursting into Cameron's eyes. He jerked the reins, putting the roan into a weaving run. Arker fired and missed. From the side, Farley sent a bullet whipping in that drew a thin streak of red across the roan's rump.

Cameron clenched his teeth against the pain beginning to surge up from his ribs. Jenny was shooting from the timber now, forcing the palomino to veer off in a wide arc. But she had no angle on Farley and he was close enough for his next shot to drop Cameron from the saddle. Carefully, Cameron laid the hot barrel of his .44 in the crook of his left elbow. He turned in the saddle and got his bead on Farley. He sought to catch the rhythm of the roan's gait, but the rocky ground made it run unevenly so that he could find no precise instant when it was best to fire.

Even so Cameron's first shot made Farley's horse break stride, made Farley's shot miss its target. Cameron fired again, coldly, deliberately, aiming now to hammer Farley out of the saddle and into the dirt. His shot caught Farley's hat, sending it sailing to one side of the trail.

Farley broke. He jerked the reins and raced wide, kicking his horse viciously. Now Larabee was coming up, his bay taking advantage of Cameron's having had to slow the roan. But the timber lay less than a dozen strides ahead. Cameron flattened himself over the saddle horn, giving Jenny a chance to shoot above him, and under the whispering of her carbine shots, he gained the shadows of the trees.

He dropped out of the saddle and jerked his carbine from the boot. Jenny stood screened by bushes and the boles of the small spruce and fir trees. Cameron joined her. He saw that Farley had rallied and the three riders were coming in abreast now, but widely spaced.

"If one of them gets in this timber, we'll be no better off than before," Cameron said. A grunt of pleasure burst from him as Jenny's shot whipped through Arker's billowing vest, sending the big man leaning to one side.

Farley was the closest to the timber, coming in from the far right. He had his carbine out now and Cameron knew that he must have glimpsed something — the whiteness of skin or the bright red of Jenny's mackinaw. He was drawing a careful bead and his horse stopped at his command.

Cameron turned and laid his carbine over a tree branch and made his sighting. Just as he fired, Farley's horse flicked its head, distracting Cameron's attention. The bullet missed its target but it caught Farley's carbine in the breech, ripping the gun from the man's hand and sending it spinning to the ground. Farley cursed wildly in shock and pain and spurred his horse back, out of range.

Jenny fired three times in rapid succession. Cameron joined her and the barrage of lead they laid down turned both the palomino and the bay, and finally Larabee and Arker had joined Farley out of carbine range.

Jenny wore man's work clothes for the man's job she was doing, but when she tilted her head and smiled at Cameron, she was pure woman. He stepped forward and their lips met briefly. Then he moved back, positioning himself to keep watch down the trail.

The three were still out of range. Arker was bandaging Farley's torn hand. Larabee's head inclined toward Arker as if he was giving an order. Then he turned the bay and rode back toward the rocks.

"He's gone after the pack animal," Cameron guessed.

"It's that man Larabee," Jenny said in a

puzzled voice. "Why does he want to kill us, Roy?"

"Me, not you," Cameron said. "He just wants you out of the way." He kept his eyes on the trail, watching Larabee return with the pack animal, watching the three men hold an obvious council of war, and finally watching Larabee ride off downtrail. At the same time, Cameron talked, telling Jenny everything that had happened since Larabee had come to town.

"Larabee's right," she whispered. "Both Balder and Stedman — and a lot of other people too — would act just the way he claims they would. Afterwards they'd start to think and they'd check up and find out the truth about you. But by then it would be far too late."

"So I know," Cameron agreed. "And I think that's why they want Tod. He overheard them talking. He might be able to show Larabee up."

She turned to watch Larabee riding away. "He's going to town now, isn't he?"

"That was his plan," Cameron said.

"Now we're stronger than they are," Jenny said. "And I know where Tod is hiding. From what you overheard about the high meadow being the one with the wild horses, he could be only one place."

She nodded uptrail. "Do you remember? The trail forks just ahead. The left fork goes to a big meadow. The right fork cuts across the mountains and drops onto the stagecoach road where it goes south out of the valley. But it's a miserable trail. Tod wouldn't have taken it because it would have left him exposed to a pursuer. There are a dozen places where he could have been shot while he was working along a ledge. I'm sure he went into the canyon and holed up in the little box canyon at the back of it."

"And the Dondees are camped in front, waiting for hunger to bring him out," Cameron said with soft bitterness. He added, "And we're not in a much better spot. If we go ahead, we run against the Dondees. If we try to ride back, Arker and Farley will stop us."

"Would you ride back with Tod up there?" she demanded.

"No," Cameron said. "Not even if the trail behind us was clear. But I was thinking of your getting back to town and warning Balder about tomorrow night."

"If I could, I wouldn't go," she said stiffly. "Your arm still isn't in any decent shape. And two against four will help Tod more than just one."

Cameron studied the trail. Arker and Farley were camped just out of gun range. Ahead, a hundred yards of open exposed land had to be crossed once they were out of the timber. Then they would have a high bluff to protect them. But the timber lay in such a way that they could not reach the bluff without crossing that open land. And once they appeared there, Arker and Farley would be after them, eager to drive them toward the Dondees waiting in the meadow.

"We can't do anything until dusk anyway," Cameron said. "Maybe then we can slip out and up to the meadow."

"Both of us," Jenny said firmly.

Cameron knew that she was right. Alone, he was no match for four men. Not in his condition. Besides, Jenny knew the country far better than he. He tried to recall the lay of the meadow, to think of a plan that would keep her as much as possible out of danger.

He knew now that none of these men would have any compunction in shooting a woman. Arker might have had at one time, but Larabee's giving him a choice — her or the gold — had made his feelings plain.

"All right," Cameron said. He looked at the sun. "It's a long time until dusk. My arm should get a good rest." He added dryly, "And a little food wouldn't hurt it either."

Jenny laughed softly. "If they can make camp, I guess we can too."

Cameron glanced at her now and then as she moved competently about, making a small camp and cooking some of the food she had brought in her saddlebags. But for the most part he kept watch on Arker and Farley, even though they showed no signs of moving.

"Larabee will have reached town by now," Jenny said later. "He'll have told his story already."

"I'll worry about that after we get Tod," Cameron said. "Right now I want you to tell me everything you know about that meadow. Draw a map if you can. We're going to have to try to trick them. Because even if we get up to the meadow without being seen by Arker, before we get out, we're going to have four men against us."

He added, "Four men here and Larabee setting up the ones in town against me."

XV

They slept, one after the other, and then they ate again. Arker and Farley remained where they were. Obviously they too were waiting for the night to come. Cameron watched the sun slide behind the distant western peaks. Now he could feel the coolness of the coming evening shadows as they reached out to probe the timber.

"In another half hour," he said warningly.

Jenny was redding up the camp. When she had everything stowed to her liking, she saddled and loaded her sorrel. Then she took Cameron's place at the watch point and he readied the roan. By now the darkness was beginning to come. In the valley, and beyond it on the sage flats, the long twilight would still be lingering. But here already the first sharp stars glittered in the indigo of the sky.

"They just built up their fire," Jenny called out. She nodded toward Arker and Farley's camp.

"That means they'll be riding soon,"

Cameron guessed. "While we keep an eye on their fire, they'll try to slip through the trees behind us."

He knelt and stirred the ashes of their small fire. Jenny had built it on a damp spot well cleared of needles and a good distance away from the nearest trees. Now Cameron blew the sparks into life and laid small pieces of dry branch on the coals.

"Let's give them something to aim for," he said. Then with a nod, he took the reins and led the roan quietly toward the trail. Jenny followed closely.

Some distance from the camp, Cameron paused. "No one can move a horse quietly through timber this thick. Let's get out on the trail before Arker hears us going."

"What if they see us?" Jenny demanded.

"Then we push the horses," Cameron said. "But my hunch is they're on the other side of the trees, trying to slip up to our camp. If so, we can get a big jump on them."

As quietly as possible, they eased the horses onto the trail. With the moon not close to rising, it was very dark here. Only the paler surface of the trail made it visible against the blackness of the forest pressing in on both sides. They continued to walk, leading the animals, seeking to make as little noise as possible. Finally they rounded the high bluff, and now they were protected from the rear. The fork in the trail lay a short distance ahead, and not far beyond that — to the left — would be the meadow.

Two shots echoed thinly from the timber they had recently left. Cameron swung into the saddle and waited until Jenny was on the sorrel. "It won't take them long to know they've been tricked," he said. "Can you lead the way?"

Jenny put the sorrel in front and let it pick its way over the rough trail. At the fork, she reined left and here the going was easier, over grass-grown ground.

Cameron felt the bold bite of the night air stiffening his muscles and he kept swiveling his right shoulder, pulling on his tender side, keeping himself loose for what lay ahead. Beyond, Jenny rounded a tight curve forced by a tall spire of rock and stopped. Cameron brought the roan alongside.

The meadow lay before them. It sprayed out fan-like, with the narrow point here and the wide end running southeast. The left side was darker than the other sides and Cameron recalled that it was a steep, timbered slope. On the right, a high wall of rock rose sheer toward the sky. It curved around to the far end, and in the far corner it was broken from some ancient upheaval.

Jenny pointed to the broken cliff face. "Tod has to be in there. It's the only hiding place."

Cameron nodded. If proof was needed, the bright point of yellow marking a small fire was enough. "The Dondees' camp," he said.

Jenny was leaning forward, straining to pierce the darkness. "I think the wild stuff is over in the far left corner," she said. "The last time I was here, I counted a dozen along with the stallion. He's a rangy dun," she added.

Cameron studied the long, gentle downward slope of the meadow. "If we ran the Dondees away long enough to get Tod out, we'd still be bottled up by Arker and Farley," he said thoughtfully. "And even if Tod is in good shape, they'd hold the high cards. What we need is some help."

"You're thinking of the broncs?" Jenny murmured.

Cameron smiled through the darkness at her. "Right. If we could use them for a screen . . ." He broke off, his smile fading. "It's a fifty-fifty chance if everything goes perfect."

"Fifty-fifty is better than what we have now," Jenny said.

Cameron nodded and leaned toward her, outlining his plan. She loosened the carbine in her saddle boot. He said, "Don't shoot except to protect yourself. Wild stock like that can get scared mighty easy. They could turn on us."

"I know how to handle broncs," Jenny reminded him quietly. Lifting her reins, she put the sorrel off the trail. Cameron watched as she worked along the left side of the meadow, following the tree line. For a time she blended into the dark timber and then she swung away from it and he could see her again in silhouette. Now he started the roan on a straight line for the yellow dot of firelight.

He kept an eye toward Jenny as he rode. When she was nearly to the dark mass they had taken for the herd of wild horses, it began to break apart nervously. Then a long-legged animal was outlined against the lighter dark of the cliff face and Cameron knew the stallion had taken wind of her. Now Jenny's sorrel quickened its pace. The stallion's head came up and his neigh shrilled through the dark night. He swung in an arc toward her, broke as the sorrel refused to give ground, and raced in the direction of the fire and the broken cliff face behind it.

Now it was Cameron's turn to act. He drove the roan forward. Jenny had her horse behind the herd, driving them on. The stallion crossed half the meadow toward the fire and then tried to veer to his right. But Cameron was there, blocking the way. With a snort of rage, the big animal swung back toward the fire.

A quick glance showed Cameron that the Dondees were up and moving toward their horses. He wondered what they must think. In this darkness, only mass movement could be seen beyond the ring of firelight. One of the Dondees shouted something, but the words were swallowed by the pounding of hoofs. Cameron lifted his arm in a signal to Jenny. She responded, letting him know she had the position she wanted. Cameron sent the roan surging forward. Once more the stallion tried to turn only to find himself blocked. And again he swung in the direction of the fire.

The Dondees were mounted now and firelight licked out, showing them waiting with their guns ready. One panicked and fired and the shot did what Cameron had expected to have to do — it sent the stallion swinging to its left, toward the only refuge it could find. It boiled into the break in the rocks. Jenny pressed hard on the small herd, driving the other eleven head after it.

"It's that girl from town!" Jupe Dondee bellowed over the hammer of hoofs. "She stampeded them on us!"

His gun lifted, catching firelight. Cameron sent a shot kicking dirt at Jupe's feet. "Hold it right there!" he snapped.

"By God, it's Cameron!" Jupe Dondee swung his gun. Cameron fired again, and this time the bullet drove Jupe's horse back in a frantic scramble. Both men lifted their arms high.

Cameron flicked his glance to the left. Jenny was following the last horse into the cut, her voice sharp and clear on the night: "It's me, Tod! It's Jenny!"

"Make it fast," Cameron cried at her. She lifted a hand and then was beyond the range of the firelight, swallowed by the darkness of the rocks.

Five minutes, Cameron thought. That should be long enough for her to see to Tod, get him out even if he had to be packed on the back of his horse.

He called to the Dondees, "Just hold it the way you are, Hale. Jupe, you toss that gun to the ground and climb off your horse. I want to see more wood on that fire, a lot more."

Jupe Dondee hurriedly obeyed Cameron's

order. Soon the fire began to blaze up, and now the two brothers were clearly outlined. Cameron danced the roan back a few steps, keeping himself on the edge of darkness.

Then a shout lifted from the far point of the meadow. Cameron turned and saw two dark forms riding hard for the fire, and he knew that five minutes was far too long. He could hold two men off with his gun, but not four. Not when he was boxed between them.

It was his plan to use the wild stock as a shield, to drive them as a wedge down the meadow until Jenny and Tod and himself could get on the trail. Then they would have a chance.

But to do this, he would have to drop to one side, picking up the drag position when the horses came into the meadow. Otherwise he would spook the stallion and send him bolting back, stampeding his herd and putting Jenny and Tod in danger of being trampled. And once he did that, he knew he would lose his position and give the Dondees a chance to use their guns.

He had counted on the stampeding horses throwing them off balance and on riding the far side of the herd which would protect him to some extent. Against two he had had a chance. Against four, he had none at all.

A voice cried, "Jupe? Hale?"

"Watch out," Hale shouted. "Cameron's here!"

A bullet whined at Cameron and he realized that he was outlined against the fire which was between himself and the break in the cliff face. He swung in the saddle and snapped two quick shots and then he sent the roan directly at the fire, swerving it at the last moment as it threatened to rebel against him. The horse made a wide swing and cut back. Bullets began to whine out of the darkness, seeking the wildly running animal and its rider.

"Gun him down!" Arker ordered. "Him and the girl both. Gun them out of the saddle!"

The Dondees spread out to block his flight and to offer Cameron only one target in any one direction. Behind him, Arker and Farley made the same maneuver. And now the four men formed a quarter circle around him, and the only opening he had left was blocked by the cliff face.

He had only one choice, and that was a small chance at best. He had to reach the break in the rocks before the Dondees closed it off against him — before one of the bullets seeking him out found its mark. He raked his heels into the roan's flanks and leaned forward, jerking the reins to make the horse run a zigzag pattern. Guns hammered from behind him and from an angle forward and to his right.

Cameron reared up in the saddle and fired, spraying his shots until he heard the click of the hammer on an empty shell. The mouth of the cut leading into the cul-de-sac where Jenny had driven the horse lay a half dozen strides ahead. Jupe Dondee was as far on the other side, riding hard to block Cameron from turning into the cut.

Cameron holstered his .44 and reached for his carbine as he saw Jupe level his gun. Rafe Arker and Hale Dondee fired at the same instant. Cameron never knew whose bullet caught him in the leg. He felt the sting and the shock. He pitched forward, grabbing for the saddle horn to keep himself from falling. At the same time he fought to hold onto the reins so that he could guide the roan.

Dead ahead and not fifteen feet away, Jupe Dondee took aim and fired.

XVI

Cameron's desperate grab for the horn threw him forward over the roan's neck. He felt the heat of Jupe's bullet as it whispered past the back of his neck, and then the mouth of the cut loomed darkly to the left.

Cameron swung the roan into that blackness and kicked with his left leg. Lead whined off rock, sending sharp shards slicing down around him. Hoofs hammered on stone as the roan caught a rock sliver and sprinted forward. The cut was a tunnel through thick rock and with not even starlight coming down from above. The blackness was complete as a bend carried Cameron out of range of the firelight.

Then the roan half-ran, half-skidded around a second bend, and two pinpricks of light appeared ahead. They resolved themselves into small fires, one on either side of the end of the cut. The roan ran between them and out onto the grass of a cliff-rimmed bowl.

He saw the wild horses huddled far to the left. On the right, against the cliff face, a third fire burned. Cameron could see two mounted figures, carbines raised.

Then Jenny cried, "Don't shoot, Tod! It's Roy!"

Cameron swung the roan toward them, brought it to a halt, and dropped to the ground. He took a single step and fell as his leg gave way.

Jenny left her sorrel and came running to him. "We tried to move the wild stuff out to help you when we heard the shooting," she said. "But the stallion won't move." She dropped down beside him. "Roy?"

"Nick in the leg," he said in thick disgust. "From the feel, the bullet went through the meat and on out." He glanced toward Tod. The boy still sat his paint pony, still gripped his carbine.

"How is he?" Cameron asked Jenny.

"Hungry and tired," she said briefly. "Let me see that leg, Roy."

He took a closer look at Tod. The boy's face was drawn, and in the firelight his eyes were sunken and brooding looking. He seemed to have gained years in the few days since Cameron had last seen him. His expression was bleak as he returned Cameron's stare.

"Are you keeping that gun for me or for

whoever might come in here?" Cameron demanded.

Tod's voice was brittle. "Which side you riding for, Roy?"

Cameron was not surprised at the question. Tod's attitude shouted suspicion, a touch of fear. "The same side I've always ridden for," he answered quietly.

"That don't tell me nothing!"

"Tod!" Jenny cried. "Stop acting like this. Put some water on to boil and get the fold of cloth from my saddlebag. Roy's leg needs tending."

"Bring the food out while you're at it," Cameron said. He made an effort to smile at Jenny. "We might as well eat. From the looks of this place, no one can get in as long as we stand guard. And it's sure we can't get out — not until that stallion calms down."

"He's spooked," Jenny agreed.

Tod hadn't moved. Cameron said softly, "Get it said, Tod. You've kept it bottled up inside long enough."

Words that Tod had obviously been twisting in his mind these past days burst out bitterly. "I heard Larabee tell how he was going to rob the bank Saturday night. I heard him say he wanted you fit to stand guard because you'd turn your back while they stole the gold!"

"That's how Larabee had it planned," Cameron agreed. "Only he forgot to ask me. When he did try to tell me how it was going to be, we had a kind of argument." He kept his voice, easy sounding. "That's why Arker and Farley are in the meadow now — to gun me down. On Larabee's orders."

"I didn't believe Larabee at first," Tod blurted out. "I thought he had some idea of putting a gun to your back, catching you off guard because you'd been beat so bad. Then I got to wondering if he didn't have some kind of hold on you. That's what Larabee made it sound like. And the more I thought about it . . ."

"And the hungrier you got," Cameron murmured understandingly.

"And then nobody came looking for me," Tod went on.

He was still on the paint, the carbine held tightly in his hand. With a resigned look, Jenny rose and went to the sorrel. She untied her gear and set it near the fire. Rummaging in her saddlebags, she brought out a fold of clean cloth. Then she put water on to boil and came back to where Cameron lay.

She said tartly, "Nobody came looking for you because we all thought you were in the hills with one of Obed's crews." Her voice sharpened. "What right do you have to think that about Roy? What has he ever done to make you believe such a thing about him?"

Tod's voice was anguished. "Why did Larabee think he could make Roy do what he wanted?"

Cameron told his story briefly, simply. While he talked Jenny slit his jeans from the knee down and laid the cloth back to expose a deep gouge in Cameron's calf. It oozed blood slowly. The bullet had obviously not stayed in him. He heard Jenny's sigh of relief.

When Cameron finished, Tod said, "You went to jail three months for something you never done?"

"For being in the wrong place at the wrong time," Cameron said. "For being friends with the wrong man."

"If you can't believe Roy, who can you believe?" Jenny demanded of Tod.

He said, "I believe him, all right. But Balder won't, nor Stedman." Tod slid from the horse and moved toward the saddlebags. Cameron noticed that even as he brought out food and prepared it, he kept his carbine handy and never put his back toward the cut.

Cameron winced as Jenny brought hot water and washed his wound. He said to Tod, "How much sleep have you had?"

"An hour now and then," Tod said. "I'd build a big fire in the middle of the trail there and get a little rest while it was burning high. The Dondees tried to come in twice. Once the fire stopped them. The other time I singed that shorter one and they stayed pretty well out." He made an effort to grin. "They kept yelling at me about the food they was eating, figuring to get me hungrier than I was. But I had a little grub with me, and I caught a couple ground squirrels and dug some roots and had me a stew."

He was plainly proud of himself and pleased with Cameron's expression of approval. He said, "There's plenty of wood on the slopes here, and all the water we need. As long as the food holds out, we can keep 'em off us."

"Of course," Jenny said. "We can sleep in shifts just as they can. It's a stand-off."

"No," Cameron said. "They hold the high cards. All they have to do is wait us out. We can't stop any bank robberies from here."

"If they're out there keeping us bottled up, how're they going to rob the bank?" Tod demanded.

Cameron said quietly, "How can we tell if they've got one man or four out there? One can hold us in here while the other three help Larabee in town. Remember, if Balder and Stedman swallow the story that I'm planning to hit the bank tomorrow night, they'll be off balance now."

Jenny said softly, "And that man Larabee is clever enough to take the gold and still blame it on you." She finished bandaging Cameron and rose. "Can you use your leg, Roy?"

Cameron got slowly to his feet. He moved slowly, stiff-legged, but he moved. He walked with Jenny to where Tod had bread and cold roast beef cut. "On a horse, I don't need the leg," Cameron said. "I wish my arm felt as sure."

"Let's do our worrying after we eat," Tod said. He wolfed down the food.

They talked little as they ate. Cameron was finishing his coffee when the moon topped the mountains and gave him his first good view of the inside of the grassy bowl. The cliffs surrounding it were high and steep, too steep for more than an occasional small tree to find dirt enough for rooting. A small stand of spruce by the spring had provided Tod with his wood. Other than that there was little but grass and glistening rock.

Tod was watching Cameron. "I looked for places to climb out," he said. "There ain't none."

Cameron looked worriedly at the rising moon. "There isn't too much time left," he said. "Larabee's making his hit at one o'clock."

"Without you there like he figured, what'll he do?" Tod wondered.

"He won't try to bull his way in," Cameron said. "He tried that once and it cost him a term in prison. Sax never makes the same mistake twice."

He thought about it. "My guess is that he'll decoy Balder and Stedman and the rest somehow and have things fixed so he can walk right up to the men standing guard. He'll take care of them and before anybody really knows what happened, the gold will be gone."

Jenny stared at the small fires by the cut. "What can we do?" she whispered. "Even if we get out now, what can we do?"

Cameron lifted himself slowly to his feet. "We ride," he said. "If we get out of here now, there's a chance of getting to town in time to do something." He nodded toward the meadow. "Unless I've got Sax figured wrong, at least two of those in the meadow will be on their way to town now to help him. If we come out of here the right way, they can't stop all of us."

Jenny was packing away the food. She looked inquiringly at Cameron. "I won't let you sacrifice yourself, Roy, just to get Tod and me free. That's foolishness. We'll find a way where we all have a chance."

"If my plan works, we'll all be safe enough," Cameron assured her. He spoke quickly, nodding now toward the wild stock huddled across the bowl, now toward the mouth of the cut.

"If there's only two of 'em out there, we got a chance," Tod said. "Forty-sixty, if everything goes right. If there's more'n two . . ."

He broke off and went quickly toward his horse. His words seemed to hang in the air as he settled himself in the saddle and waited for Cameron and Jenny to get ready.

XVII

Cameron kicked the small fires away from the entrance to the cut. Mounting the roan, he worked his right arm to make sure that the cold chill of the mountain night hadn't tightened the muscles. He could feel the pull and knew that his side was stiffening up, even as his leg was, and he said sharply, "Let's go!"

They rode across the small bowl, Jenny deliberately staying behind. Tod and Cameron swung out, skirting the rock walls, coming in one from each side on the now nervous wild stuff. The stallion lifted his head and snorted in Tod's direction. He swung about and glared at Cameron, his lip rolled back from his teeth. The mares and colts shifted nervously.

"Now!" Cameron commanded.

He sent the roan forward. On the other side, Tod did the same. Jenny appeared, dancing her sorrel in toward the stallion and cutting it quickly out again. The big horse charged this new tormentor. Jenny cracked the tip of her rope in his face, making him wheel. He was facing Tod now and his rope snapped, the end flicking the stallion's dun hide. He whinnied and dashed in the opposite direction, only to find Cameron in his way.

Now he wheeled again and ran for the only refuge — the mouth of the cut. The mares and colts streamed after him, urged by Tod's hoorawing, by Jenny's snapping rope. Cameron and Tod fell in tight behind the last mares, leaning forward in their saddles, counting on surprise to give them the moment of advantage they needed.

This was the reverse of what had happened before, Cameron thought. Only now the advantage lay with the men in the meadow, not with himself and Jenny. They would be the ones standing aside. And unless the running herd spooked their horses, they could pull back and shoot from shadow while Cameron and Tod would be outlined by the bright moonlight.

The stallion burst into the meadow, the pounding of hoofs preceding him and giving more than enough warning to anyone out there. Cameron heard a bellow over the sounds of the horses and then light from a small fire was licking at him, revealing him and Tod plainly as the stallion made an unexpected cut to the right and so drawing away any protection they might have.

"It's Cameron!" Rafe Arker shouted from darkness to the left. "And the kid!"

Lead whined across the fire, searching for Cameron and Tod. Both began to zigzag their horses, at the same time working away from the firelight. Cameron angled a little to his left, Tod to the right. As he rode, Cameron worked his gun free. He pulled the roan up suddenly and twisted himself in the saddle. Pain coursed up from his right side. He swore at the shock of it and nearly dropped his gun. Then it receded and he found the steadiness he needed.

He fired twice, turned, and sent the roan out into the meadow. "After them!" Arker bellowed. He swore in sudden surprise as the sharp sound of a carbine came from behind him.

"It's the girl!" someone shouted, and Cameron recognized the voice of Hale Dondee. Then both men were riding through the firelight. Hale twisted and fired back at Jenny.

Cameron reined the roan around and held it quiet deliberately against Arker's bullets. He drew his bead on Hale and fired. He could hear the snick of Arker's shots worrying his saddle and the rim of his hat, but rage against these men who would attack a woman drove fear out of him. He steadied the roan again as he saw his first shot miss.

The .44 bucked in Cameron's hand. Fire spewed from the muzzle and he twisted back, flattening himself over the roan's neck as the stocky horse jerked away from whining lead. A bullet searched the air where Cameron had been. He laid his gun alongside the horse's neck and shot a third time. He heard a half wild cry, cut off by the hammering of the big palomino's hoofbeats. A quick glance showed him Arker driving his horse forward on the dead run. To the left, Hale Dondee's riderless animal galloped aimlessly about.

Cameron righted himself and looked for Tod. He was moving toward the far end of the meadow as he had been instructed, and Cameron could guess how hard it must be for the boy to obey orders at a time like this.

Cameron turned back in time to see Jenny dart her sorrel up behind Arker. Her carbine lifted and steadied and she cried out a warning, wanting to make Arker turn, refusing to shoot him in the back. Arker swung the palomino and brought his gun around in a wide, sweeping movement. Cameron brought his .44 up and fired, but the big horse was weaving and the shot missed. Then Arker was on a line with Jenny and Cameron dared not fire again. Holstering his gun, he heeled the roan forward as he saw Arker's shot strike the barrel of Jenny's carbine and send it spinning out of her hands.

She cut the sorrel but the palomino moved with her, superbly as if he was working a wild cow back into a herd. Cameron realized that Arker was playing a game here — by keeping himself and his horse between Jenny and Cameron, he scotched Cameron's shooting; and by trying to catch Jenny alive instead of shooting her, he was trying to get himself a hostage. If he did, Cameron thought bitterly, then the fight was up. Larabee would win.

Cameron's only chance lay in riding Arker down. All three were close to the fire now. Cameron could see the desperation mingled with pain on Jenny's drawn features. And he could feel the eagerness radiating from Arker. He drove the roan on — fifty feet . . . thirty, Jenny made a final effort to swing the sorrel away as Arker moved to pin her in a corner of the meadow. Effortlessly, he put the palomino after her.

Cameron swung in close.

Jenny cut her horse right and then sharply left. Arker tried to match the move and the palomino lost precious feet, giving Jenny almost room enough to dart toward the open meadow. But now Cameron had the roan in close and he drove it forward with a sharp rake of his heels along its flanks.

Arker saw him when he was less than a dozen feet away. Cameron had a blurred glimpse of Arker's gun arm swinging up, of moonlight and firelight glinting off the gun barrel, and he threw himself wildly to one side. He felt the heat from the muzzle and the roar battered at his eardrums. Then he had the roan's shoulder driving against the palomino, bringing him leg to leg with Arker.

Cameron kicked himself free of the stirrups and threw his body onto Arker's, catching the heavy bulk with his left arm and letting his solid weight bring the bigger man out of the saddle. They hit the ground with Arker underneath. He grunted as Cameron drove the wind out of him. Cameron rolled and came to his feet, knowing he would last no time at all if Arker ever reached his bruised ribs.

Jenny swept the sorrel in close and

reined up. Cameron saw that she rode with one hand, having the other clamped under her armpit, and he wondered how badly the carbine had hurt her when it had been ripped out of her fingers.

He shouted, "Ride. Tod's waiting on the trail." And he turned back to Arker, who was struggling to his knees.

There was no time now for the niceties of fighting. Cameron heard Jenny send the sorrel racing away and then he moved in on Arker. He lifted a foot and drove it forward, catching the bigger man in the belly. Arker retched and went over on his side. He rolled onto his back and Cameron dropped his full weight down, pinning Arker's chest with his knees.

Arker's head was back and his mouth hung open. Cameron lifted his left arm and smashed it downward, twisting his knuckles into Arker's face. A massive hand reached up and clamped on his wrist. A fist battered his face, splitting his lips. Arker swung again, awkwardly but still powerfully. Knuckles ripped Cameron's temples and dizziness threatened to blot out his vision. He jerked his wrist free and slashed downward again. Arker rolled, taking the blow on his shoulder.

The man's stamina was unbelievable,

Cameron thought hopelessly. Now Arker's power was beginning to tell. His blows were finding Cameron's body, working closer and closer to the ribs on his right side. He caught Cameron's arm in a steel-spring grip and began to pull Cameron's body closer to his sledge of a fist.

Cameron brought his right arm up, fighting the stiffness and the surge of pain. With the last of his strength, he brought his torso around, throwing the force of its movement and weight into a driving blow. His fist caught Arker in the throat. The big man gagged and sagged away. His fingers slipped from Cameron's arm. Cameron rolled free and staggered to his feet. One of Arker's blows had laid open the skin over his eyes and he could see only dimly through a haze of blood.

Arker somehow got to his feet, still gagging and retching. His gun lay a few feet away, where it had fallen when Cameron tore him out of the saddle. He staggered in that direction and fell to his knees, shielding the gun with his body. He turned slowly, breathing raggedly through his mouth. Now the gun was clutched in both hands, and he brought it up, steadying his aim on Cameron.

"Roy!" It was Jenny's anguished voice. "Watch Rafe!"

Cameron dashed the blood from his eyes and thrust his head forward half blindly. He could make out Arker's movements, but he failed to understand their meaning until firelight glinted on the blued steel of the gun barrel. He reached for his own gun, his muscles responding with agonizing slowness. He cleared leather and brought the gun up with a sharp wrist movement. The instant before he fired, he felt his wounded leg give way. He heard Arker's shot and felt the heat of the bullet's passage. Then he crashed on his side and lay waiting, half stunned, for Arker to fire again.

He felt hands under his armpits. Jenny said, "I'll help you on the roan."

His mouth was dry and his tongue thick. "Arker?"

"He's dead. You hit him in the face. Hale Dondee's dead too."

Cameron staggered up. He saw that Jenny had her bandanna wrapped around her left hand, and that blood was seeping through.

"Get out of here," Cameron said through mashed lips. "Go with Tod and find Obed. If I'm too late getting to town, he might still catch Sax. Hurry!"

"I had to wait," she said gently. "I

Ahead and to the right, a narrow track worked up through the timber to the ridge trail. Cameron turned and walked the roan through the dark stand of trees and out into the moonlight again. The ridge trail was half covered with deadfalls and tumbles of loose rock, but there was only a short distance to go, and so Cameron let the roan set its own pace.

The trail came into town by way of Cougar Hill, dropping around a shoulder of the hill and onto Hill Street where the fancier homes were. And down where this road crossed Main, he'd find Sax Larabee, Cameron thought.

He started downslope, between rows of tall trees, riding slowly now for the sake of quietness. Cameron judged it barely short of one o'clock, and he pictured Larabee and his men moving up carefully on the sleepy guards by the bank. He could almost feel the strike of gun butts against their skulls, and he fought down an urgent need to hurry. If he hammered into town now, he would alert Larabee and lose any advantage he might have from surprise.

The better houses were gone, and smaller places lined the street now. A crossroad ahead marked the end of the lane of trees. Below that the scattered business houses began, with the hotel and bank only another block along.

Cameron reached the crossroad, paused to peer down through the empty moonlight, and lifted the reins to move on again.

A horse stepped briskly out of shadow cast by the tall trees. A voice cracked sharply, "Hold it! You've gone far enough, Roy."

Cameron turned in the saddle. Moonlight lay on Marshal Balder's tight features and it glinted off the carbine he held unswervingly, aimed at Cameron.

"So you believed Sax Larabee's story," Cameron said softly.

Balder's voice was almost sorrowful. "I had no choice. I told you I wrote to Boise for information. I got a letter back today saying you two'd been in prison together."

He brought his horse closer. "That's why I'm here. I figured Larabee was pulling a shenanigan with his talk about you hitting the bank on Sunday. I figured you'd try tonight. And I was right. Come along, Roy. You're under arrest."

XVIII

Cameron stared at the .44 aimed at him. He said softly, "So you believed Larabee's story."

"Not at first I didn't," Balder said. "And not all of it even afterward." He sounded almost sorrowful now. "I didn't want to believe it at all, but after I got that letter from Billy Rogers in Boise . . ."

With a start, Cameron recalled the letter Balder had sent to his friend in the Boise sheriff's office. "And you learned I was in prison with Sax Larabee?"

"I learned that about you and a lot more about your sidekick Larabee."

"Did the letter tell you I was released after three months when they found I was innocent?" Cameron demanded.

Balder snorted. "How many times have both of us heard that story before!" Hardness began to creep into his voice. "I thought you acted danged funny about Larabee. Then when he come to me with that story about you planning to rob the bank Sunday night, I got the idea you'd rubbed him the wrong way a little too much and he was trying to

211

get back at you. When I read the letter from Billy Rogers, I figured out what everything meant — we was supposed to sit around asleep tonight, waiting for tomorrow, while you and Larabee packed off all the gold."

Cameron started to explain and stopped before the first word was fully formed. He needed only one glance at Balder's set features to know that he would gain nothing by talking. And Balder's next words gave him proof that he was right.

"You've argued with me plenty about my claiming a jailbird don't change his stripes," the marshal said. "It looks like you proved my point instead of yours." He waggled the gun barrel. "Let's move down to the jailhouse."

"While you sit there jawing at me, Larabee's taking the gold," Cameron said in a tight voice.

Balder snorted. "I ain't as big a fool as you'd like. I figured you'd sneak into town this way and I was waiting for you. I figured too Larabee'd show up to help you at the right time — and I got two good men waiting at the bank for him." He added in a disgusted voice, "I'd have more but most everybody who came to town got liquored up early tonight."

By this Cameron judged that Obed and his crews were still in the hills, or at best at

Obed's ranch. That meant Jenny and Tod had a chance of warning Obed so that he could make a try at catching Larabee. Even if he had failed here, there was still that slim chance Jenny or Tod had got through in time.

Balder waggled his gun impatiently. Cameron said, "You might not be as big a fool as I'd like, but you're a lot bigger one than you think. Larabee isn't going to hit that bank alone. He's got Jupe Dondee and Joe Farley with him. Your guards will be looking for Larabee, not for men they've drunk with. They won't last long tonight, marshal." He glanced at the moon and added softly, "It should be about over by now."

Balder simply said, "Ride on down to the jail, Roy," in a cold, disinterested voice. Cameron did as he was bid and walked the roan in the middle of the street. He had no chance at all of getting away, he thought. Balder rode just far enough back to be safely out of reach.

Balder was a bitter man now, Cameron guessed. A man who believed he had been hoodwinked by someone he had trusted. A man who believed his judgment had been wrong. A man whose strong pride had been horsewhipped.

And he would never know how wrong he was. Even if Obed and his crew stopped

Larabee, Balder wouldn't learn the truth. Cameron knew Sax Larabee well enough to be sure he would play on Balder's belief, swear that he and Cameron together planned the robbery. He would see his chance to get his final revenge on Cameron — it was not an opportunity he would pass up.

And suddenly Cameron knew that even if he had no chance, he had to try to stop Larabee. He twisted his fingers in the reins and laid a knee into the roan's side. The sudden pressures sent it dancing backwards and to the left. Cameron jerked the reins, swinging the horse around abruptly. At the same instant, Cameron flattened in the saddle and drove his heels into the roan's flanks. The swiftness of the maneuver caught Balder off guard. He tried to jerk his own horse out of the way and at the same time bring his gun into play.

Cameron tried almost the same trick he had used against Rafe Arker. He rammed the roan's shoulder into the other horse's side. At the same time he reached out, but instead of trying to pull Balder out of the saddle, he caught the barrel of the marshal's .44 and jerked back. The gun came loose and Cameron sent it spinning to the edge of the street. He drew his own handgun awkwardly, still using his left hand.

"Don't move!" he ordered sharply as Balder lifted his heels to spur his horse. "As far as I'm concerned, we're still friends, and I don't want to hurt you."

"Be damned to you!" Balder cried.

Cameron motioned him to ride on. Balder made a sudden surge forward as if daring to find out how far Cameron would go. Cameron sent the roan after him and jerked the reins from the marshal's hand. He led the other horse to the alley and up it to the jailhouse. Here he locked Balder in one of his own cells.

His movements were slower than he liked. He wanted no lamp to warn Larabee and so he used only the moonlight that filtered into the jail. And his leg began to bother him as soon as he put weight on it. When he left the building, the clock in the office read eighteen minutes after one.

He rode on up the alley, around Mrs. Crotty's boarding house and on across the street and down the alley that ran behind Jenny's café to the rear of the bank. He rode quietly until he was even with the café. Then the roan's front hoof struck a bottle someone had thrown to the ground and the ringing sound brought shadows moving away from the bank wall ahead.

A slash of moonlight struck Jupe Dondee

and the gun he held, and Cameron knew he was too late to help the guards. He kicked the roan into swift movement, hugging dark shadow. He called out, trying to thicken his voice. "Cameron killed Arker and got loose. Tell the boss to hurry."

Jupe answered, "Hale?" in a half-suspicious voice. Then Cameron was on him. Without compunction, he came alongside and drove his gun barrel like a whip into Jupe Dondee's face. Dondee sagged in the saddle. Cameron struck again, crushing his nose, and he fell soggily to the ground.

Cameron dropped to the ground, holstered his gun and pulled his carbine from the boot. He ran limpingly toward the rear door of the bank. He almost fell over the motionless body of a man sprawled across the sill of the doorway. He stepped into the bank's backroom, a small place where the stores were kept, and he stumbled. A quick glance showed him the second guard lying where he had fallen.

A doorway ahead led into a hall and as Cameron stepped that way, he saw a faint light dancing ahead. His footsteps resounded on board flooring and Joe Farley called from up near the light: "Jupe? Who was that talking out there?"

"Hale's come," Cameron called out,

thickening his voice again. "Cameron got loose and killed Arker. We better hurry."

"Then come here and give us a hand." It was Larabee's cold incisive voice.

Cameron moved forward, the carbine resting on his hip. Someone moved in darkness ahead and the light receded. He kept going. He passed the doorway leading into the bank proper and went on toward the vault. Someone moved in that doorway and Larabee said softly, almost pleasantly, "Jupe doesn't talk quite like that, Roy. All right, Farley, take care of him."

Farley moved into view, holding a bull's-eye lantern. "Here?"

"Don't be a fool! Keep your gun on him. I don't want any shooting until we're out of town." He paused and then said quietly, "But we won't have to shoot Cameron, will we? Bring him in by the vault. I was looking for something to put against the dynamite to muffle the blast."

Farley made a gagging sound, but the gun he held was steady enough. He said, "Drop that carbine, Cameron," and when it clattered to the floor, he added, "move in there!" He took Cameron's handgun.

Cameron walked into the vault room. It was windowless and so the lamp set close to the big metal door was only partially shielded. Cameron only half believed Larabee's threat until he saw the dynamite placed strategically by the lock. He studied Sax Larabee's face and knew that the man intended to kill him this way.

"It's too bad," Cameron said dryly. "If I was to stay alive, you could think about how you broke me, how you made me lose my job and my land and maybe even my girl. This way you won't have much to remember."

"I'll have enough," Larabee said. He bobbed his head abruptly.

Cameron heard a bootsole scrape behind him and realized that Farley was coming forward to club him down. Larabee stood to one side, holding his handgun steadily, careful as always.

Cameron waited until he could feel the gusting of Farley's breath on the back of his neck. Then he dropped suddenly to one knee, pivoting on his good leg so that he faced in the opposite direction. Before Farley could make a move, Cameron drove upward. He caught Farley in the belly with his shoulder, spun him toward Larabee and pushed.

Larabee was setting for a shot and he tried too late to check himself. His bullet slammed into Farley and his staggering body suddenly went limp. Cameron heard Farley's gun hit the floor. He dropped to one knee. His fingers closed over the gun butt. He jerked the .44 up, lifting his head at the same time.

The force of Farley's body drove Larabee backwards. He caught himself and pushed the heavy weight to one side. He seemed to sense that he had no time to aim at Cameron. His gun whipped toward the lantern. He fell away as he fired. Cameron's shot shattered only darkness as Larabee's bullet smashed out the light.

Cameron could hear Larabee's soft breathing, and then that was curbed, leaving only silence. Cameron tried to orient himself to the doorway, but the door had been closed when Farley brought him in and there was nothing to see except thick blackness.

Bootsoles scraped over the floor. Cameron swung in the direction of the sound. It stopped and a moment later started again well to the left of the point Cameron had located it. Puzzled, he tried to guess what Sax Larabee was up to, tried to keep up with that quick, deadly brain.

A match flared. Something hissed. Cameron swung toward the sound and the faint glow that showed as the match puffed out. He turned around at the noise of the door opening. Then it slammed shut and the latch dropped down.

From the other side of the door, Sax Larabee called softly, "That's a short fuse I lit, Roy. Go put it out if you have time."

What foolishness was this? The burning fuse was less than the room's width from him — a half dozen strides at the most. Cameron got to his feet and stepped toward the dull reddish pinpoint of light. He was no more than a step away when he heard the door latch lift. He jumped back instead of forward. From the doorway, Larabee's gun blasted viciously and his bullet struck the floor where Cameron would have been standing had he tried to put out the fuse.

Cameron lost his balance as his bad leg gave way. He tried to turn as he fell, to bring his gun up, to get a shot at Larabee. The door slammed shut again.

"Next time," Larabee called. "How long is the fuse now, Roy?"

Acrid smoke drifted to Cameron's nostrils now. The light from the burning fuse beckoned to him mockingly. He felt sweat break out on his body and the hand holding Farley's gun trembled.

How did you best a man who could think as swiftly as Larabee did? A man who could wait coolly beyond that door, knowing the shots would bring townsmen, but willing to take the risk, willing to lose the gold for the sake of gaining his revenge?

Cameron could see only the burning end of the fuse. The light was too thin to tell him how far it was from the dull glow to the dynamite. He might have five minutes. He might have only five seconds. He moved to his left, scraping his bootsoles heavily over the floor, hoping to draw Larabee into opening the door.

"You aren't going in the right direction, Roy. You're only wasting precious time."

Cameron moved again, this time toward the sound of Larabee's voice, toward the doorway. He felt his foot hit something yielding and he pitched forward, dropping the gun. He found a match in his pocket and struck it alight. The gun lay beside Farley's dead body.

He heard the door come open and he sought to blow out the match and to roll away at the same time. Larabee's gun smashed into the darkness. Cameron felt the whip of the bullet and heard it probe soggily into Farley. Then the door slammed again.

He had rolled on the match and there was only the dull glow from the fuse. But that second shot seemed to have jarred his brain. He spent precious seconds examining a sudden idea. Then he went on his knees back to Farley's body. He lifted it and maneuvered until he had Farley's arms draped around his neck and Farley's chest and belly pressed against his back.

With Farley covering his back like clammy armor plate, he dragged himself across the floor toward the burning fuse. He made no effort to be quiet except to hold the .44 up from the rough boards. The reddish glow was some distance from where it had been before, and as Cameron neared the light was strong enough for him to see faint reflection from the metal of the vault.

The door came open. Larabee fired. Cameron felt the jar of the bullet striking into Farley's body. Then the gun butt smashed down on the burning end of the fuse. The faint light died.

Larabee fired again and again the bullet struck Farley's body. Cameron straightened up suddenly so that the body slid to one side. He turned, bringing the .44 around in a sweeping motion. His eyes focused on the door frame as it outlined faint light seeping down the hallway. They focused on the thin darkness of Larabee standing sideways, framed by that light.

A gout of flame stabbed out toward Cameron. The .44 bucked in his hand. He heard a startled cry from Larabee, a gasp of surprise and disbelief. Then the sound was cut off abruptly as something smashed at his shoulder, driving him to the floor. A roaring filled his ears, and for an instant he thought he had missed the burning fuse and the dynamite had gone off. Then he had no thoughts at all. Only darkness filled his mind.

Doctor Draper said with sour humor, "I told you the other day that you wouldn't be up and around for a while yet, Roy."

Cameron could see the doctor's thin face looming over him. Beyond it, he caught the warm glow of Jenny's eyes. The face moved away and Jenny came closer. She touched his fingers with her own.

"How long have I been here this time?" Cameron asked. His voice sounded rusty to his ears.

"It's noon Monday," Jenny answered. She brushed him with her smile. "But you're all right, Roy. The bullet's out and the doctor says the wound is clean."

"You're tough!" Draper snapped. He scowled as if he found his own diagnosis hard to believe. "Torn ligaments, two bullet holes in you . . ." He broke off and went out of the room.

Cameron said worriedly, "Balder — I left him in a cell!"

"Tod and I found him when we came to town with Obed about three o'clock Sunday morning. He said he'd heard shooting from the bank and we went there and found you."

Cameron said bitterly, "I had to lock Balder up. He thought I was in with Larabee and tried to jail me."

"He doesn't think it anymore," she said softly. "Not after he heard Tod's story and mine — and Jupe Dondee's. He's still alive and he did a lot of talking." She smiled. "The marshal seemed almost pleased to have been wrong about you."

Her smile broadened. "The former marshal, that is. The job is yours when you're ready for it, Roy."

"You're talking too much," Cameron said. "How can I kiss a woman who's talking all the time?"

She laughed and bent toward him. Their lips touched. She drew away. "Are you going to do that every time I try to talk?"

"Every time."

"In that case," she said, "I'll plan on a lot of talking."